Dangerous Bet:

Troy's Revenge

Tycoon Club Series: Book 1

By

Marie Rochelle

This is a work of fiction. Names, characters, places, and incidents are products of the author's imagination or are used fictitiously and are not to be construed as real. Any resemblance to actual events, locales, organizations, or persons, living or dead, is entirely coincidental.

Troy's Revenge by Marie Rochelle
Red Rose Publishing
Copyright© 2007 Marie Rochelle
ISBN: 978-1-60435-900-8
Cover Artist: Nikita Gordyn
Editor: Savannah Grey

Red Rose Publishing
www.redrosepublishing.com
Forestport, NY 13338

Dedication:

To all of my fans. Thanks so much for always supporting my work. All of you are the best.

Marie

Chapter One

"I'm not going to let you get away with this. I knew that you hated my family, but I never thought it ran this deep. Tell me what I've got to do to get it back."

Troy Christian leaned forward in his seat and drummed his fingers on the glossy surface of his desk. It didn't even take twenty-four hours before she came to him. He knew that she would once she found out what he had done to her family.

"Headley, I don't why you're here. You know that your father signed those papers in good faith and I can't do anything about it. Now, I think you should leave before you say something that can't be taken back."

Storming across the room, Headley Rose slammed her purse down on the desk and glared at him so hard that he almost flinched in his chair, but stopped in the nick of time.

"I could care less if I said something to hurt your feelings. You're so damn cold that you probably have a hole where your heart should be. My father worked himself into that hospital bed for that ranch and now you're taking it away without a second thought."

Troy brushed off Headley's comment without blinking an eye. He understood that the young woman was mad at him, but she had no right to be.

Instead of running off and trying to be a fashion designer in New York, she should have stayed and helped her father with their business.

"Douglas came to me for help and I helped him. Why should I be blamed because he couldn't make the payments? I'm a businessman and I have

6

a right to take what's mine." Troy commented watching as Headley's gorgeous eyes darkened in anger.

"You're a bastard. I hope you know that. You've so much money that you could give millions away and not even feel it. My dad kept that place going after mom died so he wouldn't lose his mind. You even came to the funeral and offered your support. Now, I see it was all part of your plan."

"What plan?" Troy asked, not liking the turn that this conservation was taking.

"For years the men in your family have been pissed that my father got the land you wanted. In fact, they tried trying various ways to get it from him. So, you befriended my dad and made him think you were on his side until the right time came along to stab him in the back. But I promise you, this isn't going to work."

"God, for all I know my father didn't have a heart attack while he was repairing that fence. You could have done something to him," Headley accused shocking the hell out of him.

Jumping up from his seat, Troy raced around his desk to grab Headley by the arm jerking her to his body.

"Listen here, little girl," he growled. "I don't try to kill people to get what I want. I was the one who found Douglas out there and got him to the hospital. If it wasn't for me, your father would be dead."

"That's what you say. How do I know it isn't a lie? I remember quite clearly before I left that you told my father you wouldn't let him sell that property to anyone but you, Mr. Christian."

"You shouldn't accuse me of doing something that you've no proof of. I'm tired of telling you that you're wrong. Furthermore, you might not like what happens if you keep it up."

8

Titling her head back, Headley looked him in directly in the eye without flinching. "What can you do to me? I'm not scared of you."

I could kiss the hell out of you like I've wanted to do since you walked into this office, Troy thought before let go of Headley's arm and stepped back.

"Nothing, just go to the hospital and check on Douglas. I'll talk to you later about a way to work something out about the payments."

Headley picked her purse up off the desktop and stared at him. "I'm not going to set up any payment arrangements with you. I'll find a way to have my father's debt paid off before he gets out of the hospital at the end of the month," she promised then headed towards the door.

He didn't like the sound of that. Headley had always been headstrong and he was worried about what she would do to get the money. "Your father owes me close to fifty thousand dollars. There's no way you can get that paid off in time."

"I bet I can," Headley promised before she stormed out the door, slamming it behind her.

Headley made herself not think about Troy again until she came back from the hospital and was in her old room back at the ranch.

How in the hell could he still be so damn gorgeous after so many years? His jet black hair was still thick and full despite the fact that he was nearly thirty-two years old. In addition, the gray hairs that were streaked throughout only made him sexier and more desirable.

What was wrong with her, still lusting after the man who wanted to ruin what was the life of her family business? Rose Ranch had been the best in its time until Troy's family moved into town when she was young.

She would never forget how the older girls in town constantly found ways to draw Troy's piercing blue eyes in their direction. If she remembered correctly, he was about twenty-two when they moved to the land across from hers.

She was still in high school and secretly lusted for him herself, but never let on to any of her friends. *Why would she?* Troy was already six years older than her with had a line of willingly girls waiting for him.

In ways, even back then, her father and his family weren't getting along at all. Troy's dad didn't like having competition for his ranch and tried several times to buy theirs, but her father always told them no. It wasn't for sale.

Things only got worse when her mother died during childbirth along with her baby brother. He father went into a deep depression and never fully came out of it.

She had sat beside him at the funeral, in shock, trying to stay strong while he cried. A light touch on her leg had made her look up and to find Troy squatting down in front of her with a sad look on his face. She was so taken back all she could do was stare at him. He had never shown her any attention until that day.

"Are you okay?" He asked with genuine concern in his deep voice. "Can I help you with anything?"

"No," she finally replied when she gained her voice. "I'm fine, but I'm worried about Dad. He's taking all of this very hard."

"Give him some time. The pain will pass. I was the same way when my mother died. I never thought it would get easier, but it did." Leaning forward, he planted a kiss on her cheek that almost made her faint on the spot. "Please call or come over if you need to talk. I'll be glad to listen," he whispered in her ear. Giving her leg one last squeeze, Troy had gotten up and left the service.

"Why did I ever think back then that he was a nice guy? Men who look like him are always for themselves and nothing else," Headley complained to herself as she changed her clothes and climbed into bed. "Well, I'm not going to let him win this battle. He's not going to take this place away from my father."

Turning off the light, she turned on her side and tried to get some sleep without thoughts of the dangerously sexy Troy Christian in her head.

Chapter Two

"Mr. Christian, is everything okay this morning? You seem a little preoccupied. Is there anything I can do for you?"

Troy dropped his fingers from his temple to found his secretary standing in front of his office desk with several folders in her hand. He didn't even know how long she had been standing there. He couldn't get his mind off the fact that Headley had bet him she could have the entire amount of money her father owed back to him in a matter of weeks. What in the hell was she going to do to get her father's debt paid in full?

"Mr. Christian," his secretary's voice chimed in again.

"Heather, I'm fine. Please just lay the files on my desk and go to lunch. There's no need to worry about me." He answered making eye contact with her.

Troy hoped that Heather would leave without asking him any more questions. He should have stayed home and worked from the ranch like he wanted to this morning. But he hadn't been into the office for about a week and he felt the urge to check in.

"Yes, sir," Heather replied, placing the information down like he requested. Then she left closing the door behind her.

Picking up the file on the top, he flipped it open and read over the contract in his hand. He hadn't tricked Douglas into signing this agreement. Headley's father had come to him looking for help and he had given it to him, but with a deadline attached. Douglas promised him that he would have the money back within a two-year period, but he failed to live up to his end of the bargain.

How could Headley even think that he would do something to harm her father? Douglas Rose was a good, honest, hardworking man. For as long as he had known the man, Douglas had never asked for a hand-out. Then the ranch started losing money when bad weather and droughts hit not to mention the bad investments and his heavy drinking.

But he wasn't about to lose money. Not for anyone, not even Headley. He still couldn't believe how stunning she was. A day didn't go by that he didn't think about those huge dark brown eyes of hers or the hourglass shaped body that he had wanted and desired since he and his family moved to this town.

Headley was a constant temptation to him from the moment he saw her running down the trail at her house. He had been out riding and was coming back in when he saw her everything around him stopped.

His cock had grown so hard, making it impossible to sit comfortably on his horse. She was a vision of perfection with the way her young, perky breasts bounced underneath her white t-shirt. The matching shorts had shown off her perfect Hershey's kiss chocolate skin making ideas he shouldn't be thinking about popped into his twenty-two year old head.

Instead of following her, like his body and mind pushed him to do, he turned and headed back for his house. He had made sure no one was home before he locked himself in his room to give his body the relief it craved.

Headley had been so young that she never realized how badly he wanted her back then. Hell, the need hadn't left him even after all of these years. His body still wanted hers with a driving need that made his gut clench. It didn't even stop when she stormed into his den looking madder than hell and ready to slap the taste out of his mouth.

It was quite a change from the quiet and shy girl that left here looking for fame in the high paced fashion industry. He'd never forget the day he had followed Headley's family to the bus station and watched her leave his life. It was the worst pain he had ever felt, but he never let anyone know. His feelings for Headley were private and no one else needed to know about them.

"I see you're sitting there plotting how to bring down another family," a feminine voice uttered from the doorway.

Troy slowly replaced the paper back into the folder and closed it. "I'm glad to see you got my message that I left on your answering machine last night. I was a little concerned you might not show up." He replied watching as Headley came into his office oblivious to the fact that he wanted to kiss her senseless.

"Your message wasn't a request, but a demand. How could I not come? You know that I want to save my father's business as soon as I can and head back to New York. So, what do you want?"

Headley was going to leave?

Troy didn't like the sound of that. He'd have to find a way to make her stay here with him and if he had to use her father to do that, then so be it. "You made a bet with me last night that you'd find a way to pay off Douglas's off in full. I think it's only fair that you know the entire amount. I don't want you making a bet that you won't have the ability to keep. Besides, making a bet with a man like me is a dangerous thing because I always play to win," he grinned.

"You're so damn cocky. It makes me sick. Now, tell me what I need to know. I've places to go and people to see."

"What's the hurry Headley? We're going to be seeing a lot of each other since you owe me money. When it comes to money, I don't play." Troy stood up and made his way around the edge of his desk. Sitting on the side, he waved his hand towards the empty seat in front of him. "Have a seat. We have to discuss a few things."

Headley's black spiral curls bounced off her shoulder as she came across the room and fell down into the seat. "Don't waste my time."

"What happened to make you so demanding? You used to be so patient and laid-back when you were growing up. Did the tough life of New York make you hard?" Troy inquired.

"I was still the same person until I got Dad's letter and he told me how you're trying to steal the ranch from him."

"We've had this conversation before. I'm not a thief or a crook. Douglas got into this trouble because he made bad investments after you left and not even the bank would loan him money. You should be thanking me for helping your father instead of trying to shove the blame on me."

"My dad knew how to run that ranch with one hand tied behind his back. You're lying about him. He would never waste the ranch's money like that." Headley tossed back.

"Alcoholics seldom know right from wrong when a bottle is involved. Douglas changed a lot after you abandoned him to ran off chasing after a foolish dream. Everyone thought you would stay here and work side by side with him. But no, Headley Rose was too caught up in leaving and making her own mark in the world to care about her father."

"You're a *damn* liar. My father never had an addiction a day in his life. You just want me to believe these lies about him," Headley shouted, standing up. 'But I'm not going to listen to this.

Dad is a good man and nothing you say will make me think otherwise."

"Sit down," Troy uttered pushing Headley back down in the chair. He wasn't going to let her keep living in the past. Douglas Rose wasn't the father had she left over ten years ago. He had changed, and it wasn't for the better.

Reaching behind him, he picked up the folder and shoved it under Headley's face. "Look at this and tell me your father's debt isn't more than you can repay." He couldn't let her shoulder the weight of this. He wanted the money back, but not at the expense of her making a deal, she had no way in hell of keeping.

"How do I know these aren't something you had fixed up to trick me?" She asked, snatching the folder out of his hand.

"God, woman," he growled. "I'm trying to help you out here. Do you know how many people wished I would give them this kind of deal?"

"I've read about you in business magazines over the years. What's the nickname they gave you?" She asked, standing back up so they were eye level, "Yeah, the devil in an Armani suit. Some men and women would sell their soul for a moment of your time, but I'm not one of them."

"Headley, don't make me prove how true that nickname came be. I want to help you, but if you keep punching my buttons, you'll lose. I've a lot more experience that you when it comes to this world. I consider you a friend. However, one more insult and I might forget that you are."

"Mr. Christian, don't worry about it. I've given you alot of names over the years, but friend isn't one of them. I'm going to take this back home and read it, but it won't make any difference. I bet you that I'll get my father's balance to you paid off and I will."

She tried to slip by his body, but Troy was tired of Headley and her smart tongue. Grabbing her by the arm, he pulled her back against his body until not an inch separated them. "That smart mouth of yours is going to get you in a world of trouble one day. You should learn how to control it."

"I'll worry about that when the time comes. Right now, I'm only worried about getting you out of my father's life," she retorted

"How do you know now isn't the time? I might be the one who'll teach you to use that tongue of yours for more pleasurable things." Troy's voice whispered as he trailed his finger over Headley's bottom lip. He heard her breath catch and a smile pulled at the corner of his mouth. "I see that you aren't as immune to me as you pretend to be. Don't you want me to kiss you?"

Twisting her head away, Headley moved his finger from her mouth. "You're not going to do this to me. I won't let you. You might have used my father to get what you wanted, but I'm not going to fall for it."

Without giving her a chance to react, he covered Headley's sinful mouth with his and thrust his tongue inside.

He was tired of hearing her bad mouth him. He had warned her about what would happen if she didn't stop. Now it was time for Headley learn what trouble she could get into when she didn't listen.

Chapter Three

Desperately, Headley tried to listen to the voice screaming in the back of her mind to push Troy away, but it was as if her arms wouldn't work. A part of her hated the fact that Troy was kissing her. However, the other half *loved* it. All of her secret fantasies were coming true.

The slow stroking of his tongue inside her mouth sent tiny tremors through her body. Little by little, her traitorous body was turning into a puddle of mush.

Why did she have to want the man who was single handedly trying to take away her family's legacy? No, she couldn't let this happen...not *with* Troy Christian of all people.

"Let me help you," his warm breath whispered against her mouth. 'You can't handle

Douglas' problems by yourself. It's too much for you. You need me and we both know it."

You need me!!!!! Those words were all Headley heard in her head and it only took her a split second to react. Placing her hands on Troy's warm, hard chest, she shoved him away until there was space between their bodies.

"No, I don't need your help. Your interference is what got my father into this mess in the first place," she snapped.

Wiping the back of her hand across her mouth, Headley stepped away from Troy. She couldn't let him see how badly his kiss had bothered her. He already had the upper hand. It wouldn't do her any good for him to get another advantage over her.

"I'm not going to say this again. Stop kissing me. I don't like it," she lied, hoping that Troy didn't notice how fast her heart was beating through her shirt.

If he knew how much further she truly wanted to take that one little kiss, she'd be in real trouble. Without a doubt, she knew he would have kissed her again and would not have stopped until they both got what they desired. She watched as Troy moved around his desk and took a seat on the edge.

He was so damn sexy! How was it possible for one man to look this good after so many years? She was such a liar. She did want him.

However, she couldn't let her emotions control her. Troy wouldn't seduce her with stolen touches here and there into getting what he wanted. This was business between them and nothing else.

She wasn't a sixteen year old girl anymore, in love with her gorgeous neighbor across the field. She was a grown ass woman who had come home to help her sick father out of this horrible situation. After everything was taken care of, she was going back to New York.

"Headley...." Troy uttered as he slid off the corner of his desk and slowly sauntered towards her, but stopped mere inches from her throbbing body. His eyes were so intense, they resembled shining sapphires.

"I mean it," she hissed, stepping back until her legs hit the back of a table in the middle of the room. "Keep your lips, hands or any other part of your body off mine."

Troy's eyes narrowed on her face. "Fine, I'll never force my lips or any other part of my body on you again, Ms. Rose." He flung back. "All you'll get from me now is a handshake after I get the hundred thousand dollars you owe me."

Headley barely caught herself in time before she almost fainted. That wasn't the amount he had given her earlier. How in the hell did the amount jump up like that? What in the hell kind of game was he playing with her?

"I've said it before and I'll say it again, there's no way he owes you that much money. Hell, you keep making the price of his debt higher and higher. I know for sure now you aren't being a hundred percent honest with me."

Without the slightest warning, Troy closed the remaining distance between them and her breath caught in her throat. She didn't know what he was going to do next. He looked pissed and ready for a battle.

From the unblinking stare that he was giving her, it couldn't be good. She was more than nervous that Troy might ignore her warning, because if he placed those sculptured lips of his on her mouth this time, she wouldn't be able to tell him no.

Headley tried to swallow, but Troy was so close that she couldn't even breathe. The scent of his aftershave was doing things to her body that were probably illegal in some states.

"Princess, I've warned you about saying things that you can't take back," Troy whispered running his finger down the side of her neck. "Most people would do practically anything to get out of that kind of arrears."

"I don't have any other choice but to do what I've got to in order to save my father's business." Headley muttered and then gasped when Troy's fingers toyed with the buttons on her sweater.

In the back of her mind, she wondered if Troy sensed her hidden attraction to him. She doubted that he did because, being the devil he was, Troy would use it to his advantage. He was just messing with her and they both knew it.

"We all have choices but making the right choice is usually the problem," he answered, stepping away from her and taking his body heat with him. "Are you ready to make the right one?"

"What are you talking about?" Headley responded.

Walking away from her, Troy went back over to his desk and took his seat behind it. He leaned back in the seat, propped his feet up and crossed his ankles on the smooth surface. "You've bet me on numerous occasions that you'll have Douglas' debt paid off, but you haven't heard my terms. If you don't have my money by the agreed date, are you ready to hear my side of the bet?"

"Terms...what terms?"

"Headley, a bet usually has two sides: a winner and a loser," Troy chuckled crossing his hands. "I've heard your side, now it's time for you to hear mine."

Headley wanted with everything in her to tell Troy where he could go, but she couldn't.

Her father was still in the hospital and the doctors didn't know when he was going to wake up. It went without saying that he wouldn't be able to clean up this mess without her help.

However, she got the feeling whatever Troy was about to tell her would change the rest of her life.

"I'm ready for anything you're going to toss my way," Headley said with more bravado that she actually felt.

He gave her a smug smile that shouldn't have sent her pulse racing, but did. "Alright, Ms. Rose. My end of the bet is that if you lose and can't pay the amount in full back, you've got to marry me."

Troy sat in silence while a display of emotions from surprise to utter horror passed across Headley's beautiful face. He didn't know if he should accept her reaction or be pissed that the thought of being married to him disgusted her that badly.

Shit, he was a *damn* good catch. Half the women in Paris, Texas wanted to be with him. Headley should be thrilled that he had proposed marriage in the first place.

She was being too silent. This just wasn't the vocal woman he knew and secretly loved. He had to find out what was going on in that head of hers.

"What, no flippant comment?" He taunted. "I was expecting more out of you."

"You can't be serious. Why would you ever think I would marry you? We haven't done anything but fight since I came back to town," Headley gasped; stunned that Troy would even bring up such a suggestion.

"I'm dead serious, Headley. I need a woman in my home, life and bed. I think you would be the perfect choice. I wouldn't have to worry about you begging for my attention all the time. Plus, a small part of me wants to stick it to you."

Headley was having a hard time processing all of this. Why did Troy want to get back at her? What had she ever done to him? Lord....she hadn't even been in his presence for over ten years.

"Stick it to me...that doesn't make any sense. I've never done anything to you."

"Oh, but you did," Troy growled. "You walked around town like you were too good to even speak to me. When you were with your friends and saw me coming towards you, you would turn and walk the other way. I might have been older than you, but it still hurt."

Did Troy *really* not know the reasons behind her sudden departure all those times? Surely, he had to have known that she had fantasies about him. All of her friends would tease her constantly about her feelings for her sexy, older neighbor.

"Headley, are you paying attention to me?" he snapped.

"Yeah, I'm listening, but I'm not liking what I'm hearing," Headley tossed back. "I'm not going to agree to this. You can take you offer and shove it up your conceited ass."

"Have I told you how much I love a passionate woman?" Troy asked, dropping his feet back down on the floor. "You're going to take my offer because you aren't going to have any other choice. I'll give you until the end of the month to get me my money, but I know you won't. So, you better be ready to have a wedding in your future."

She wasn't going to let Troy bully her into this, no matter how many times she dreamt of what it would be like to have a relationship with him. He had to understand that he couldn't always get what he wanted by threatening people. It might work on most of the people he knew, but it wasn't about to work on her.

"I don't think so. I'm not ever going to be Mrs. Troy Christian and the sooner you realize that, the better off you'll be."

"You love challenging me, don't you?" Troy inquired, getting up from his seat. "I've never been a man who has backed down from anything in my life. I love conquering new things, and Headley, I want to take control of you."

He wouldn't have to try that hard to make me fall for him, she thought. *I'm halfway there already*.

"Keep dreaming, Troy." She tossed back, hoping she came off calmer than she felt. "Like I said, there won't be a marriage between us. I'll make sure of it."

Troy gave her a predatory smile as he strolled towards her. "Do you know what I'm going to do on our honeymoon?" He asked, pausing an arm's length away from her body.

"No....what?" she whispered, anticipating what Troy was about to tell her.

"I'm going to kiss you until the only thing you can do is say yes, Troy. You won't have the strength to fight me about anything after I finish making love to you. Now, go on, try to win your side of the bet. However, I've no doubt in my mind that I'm going to win."

Headley's body heated up at Troy's challenge. Why was she so attracted to the bad boy...no man in front of her? One thing about Troy, he was a GROWN ASS man and he knew it.

For years she couldn't keep a man in her life because she compared them to the image of Troy she keep in her mind. *God...how was she ever going to be able to get through this bet?* She couldn't let him know how much she wanted him.

Troy fed on dominating people and she couldn't let him have that ultimate power over her. He was so perfect in so many ways, but she had to stay focused and get her father out of this mess and rush back to New York as fast as she could.

"What makes you think that I don't already have a boyfriend waiting back for me in New York?" She tossed out, trying to save what part of her senses that she had left.

"I know for a fact that you don't."

"You seem awful smug with your answer," Headley commented. "I could have a boyfriend and all of this would have been for nothing."

"I'm so smug because I know that if you were my woman, I wouldn't let you leave New York and come all the way to Paris without me."

"I'm not a piece of property that anyone owns. I can come and go as I please."

"Yeah....you say that now because you haven't found a man you can't be without," Troy stated. "But once we're married, you won't be able to go anywhere alone because you'll always want me at your side."

Headley couldn't believe that Troy had such little faith in her. She was going to get the money back to him with time to spare. He was going to eat the words he just said to her. Troy was ruthless when it came to business, but she was just as ruthless when it came to her father.

"You're mouth has a lot to say, but most of it is worth nothing. Can't you find something better to do with it than taunted me?"

She realized her mistake a second too late as Troy reached out and yanked her into his arms, quickly covering her mouth with his. His lips were hard and searching while his tongue explored the recess of her mouth.

Headley wanted to fight, but she couldn't. The kiss was sending the pit of her stomach into a whirlwind, like she was on a roller coaster ride and she didn't want to get off. It had been such a long time since her body had got turned on from just a mere kiss.

"Stop fighting this," Troy's breath whispered against her mouth. "We both know that you want me. Just succumb to me, and I promise that I can wipe every other man from your memory."

Grabbing her hips, Troy yanked her tight against his body as his cock pressed into her stomach, demanding attention. "I've never been this hard for another woman. Let me have you. Stop being so strong willed. We'll be so good together plus once we get married, Douglas' debt will be paid in full."

Headley's body flinched as if she had been doused with cold water. She couldn't believe the words that just came out of Troy's mouth. He thought she would have sex with him just to get rid of her father's problems. *What in the hell was wrong with him?*

A suffocating sensation tightened her throat as she shoved Troy away from her. She shouldn't blame him for thinking she would give in to him when he offered her some sex. It wasn't like women him off when he kissed them.. He was probably used to charming his way into a woman's bed, but she couldn't let herself become one of them.

She had come home to take care of business and nothing else. "I wouldn't book the church if I were you, because you aren't going to win. I'll take your bet and I'm very confident things will work out in my favor."

Going around his body, Headley snatched the file Troy had given her up off his desk and made her way towards the door. She was halfway out the door when Troy's deep voice yelled behind her, "I want you to wear white on our wedding day."

Headley's steps didn't falter as she hurried for the elevator because all she could think about was how she had to win this bet at all costs. There was no way in *hell* that she could become Mrs. Troy Christian.

Chapter Four

"Hey daddy, how are you doing today?" Headley asked as she took a seat in the chair by her father's bed. Placing her hand on top of his, she tried not to cry, as Douglas Rose didn't answer her. The doctors had warned her before she came in that her father was still in a coma, but she didn't want to believe it.

After her trying day with Troy yesterday, she wanted some good news, but it didn't seem like she was going to get any here. It pained her to see her strong father connected to all of those tubes.

Her father didn't look his seventy-six years at all. Jet black curly hair covered his head with just a hint of gray in it. His face was strong without a wrinkle to show his true age. She remembered how her mother used to tease her father unmercifully about how he took care of himself by working out six days a week and used sunscreen anytime he went out to work with the other ranch hands.

Tears welled up in her eyes at the thought of losing her last living parent.

She hadn't been able to keep in close touch with her dad over the years because of her job, but she never missed calling him on his birthday or all the holidays. Why hadn't he told her that he needed money? Douglas was never a man who asked for help, so what made him go to Troy for help?

"Daddy, I know that you can hear me. You've got to be able to hear me. I'm going to get you out of this mess. I won't let Troy win."

Leaning over, Headley placed a kiss on her father's cheek. "Listen, I've got to go and see about getting a job. I don't have enough money in my savings to completely pay off Troy, but I'm going to get a job while I'm here. So, when you wake up, you won't have anything to worry about except getting better."

She squeezed her father's hand one last time and quickly stood up. It was so hard for her to see her father, who was once so full of life, lying so still in this hospital bed. Despite what Troy said, she knew he had a hand in this and she so disappointed in herself for responding to his kiss yesterday. No...regret wasn't the right word, she felt downright guilty.

"Okay...enough of this. I've got to take control and get this done. Troy may be a tycoon, but neither his money nor his power is going to make me bend," she swore as she left her father's hospital room.

"Tommy, I swear I can do this job. Come on, we've known each other since third grade. I need money and I know this job will help me save it up faster. I don't mind working the late hours."

"I'm not sure about this," Tommy Cook sighed, drumming his fingers against the bar countertop. "I got this club because of Troy. I don't want to get on his bad side. He could close me down for helping you. I still have two more payments on the money I borrowed from him."

"See...that's what I'm talking about," Headley snapped. "Troy uses his power to make people scared of him. He did that to my father, and now he's in a hospital bed."

"Surely you aren't suggesting that Troy put Douglas in that room. God...Headley, Troy was always the one who came and picked up your father when he had one too many beers. Troy is a good man. Yeah, he can be a little hard at times, but when someone needs help, he's there for them."

"Stop calling my father a drunk. You're sounding like Troy. My dad wouldn't turn to liquor to solve his problems. I don't want to hear about this anymore. Do I have the job or not?"

"Headley, you're too overqualified to be a waitress....but I do need the help," Tommy sighed looking at her. "When can you start?"

"Can I start tonight?" Headley asked standing up from her seat. "Let me go home and change clothes, and I'll be right back."

"I know I'm making a big mistake by doing this," Tommy sighed. "But yeah, you can start tonight. Stop at the bar and Fancy will give you a t-shirt."

"You still worry way too much," Headley grinned, excited about finally being able to make more money. "Everything is going to turn out perfect! I'm going to get the extra money I need for

Troy and you're getting a new sexy waitress for your gentleman's club."

"If you say so," Tommy muttered, unsure.

"I know so." Headley retorted pleased that something was finally going her way.

"I think that we need to go to the club tonight and get our minds off of work," Maxwell Reed stated before taking another sip of his brandy. "I want to see what hot new girl Tommy has working for him."

"I don't have time for the club tonight," Troy muttered. "I have more important things to take care of." He didn't understand why Maxwell wasted so much time at the Tycoon's club in the first place. If the god awful name wasn't enough to keep him away, the woman there should be. All they wanted to do was land a rich man to take care of them. He had grown too old for that crowd now. He only had two interests at the moment. One was winning the bet over the delectable Headley Rose and the other was finding a way to get her into his bed.

She had been stunning when she was younger with her curves and more than a handful breasts. But now, she had matured into a beauty. He wanted her...BAD!

He wasn't going to stop until she couldn't find a way to repay the money Douglas owed him. He was going to get back at her for leaving him all those years ago without even a goodbye. He didn't care that Headley never knew how he felt about her. She had no right to tear his heart out of his chest. Now, it was his turn to give her a taste of her own medicine.

"Could one of those important things be named Headley Rose?" Maxwell chuckled. "Man, I saw her in town today and she was smoking hot. I wouldn't mind having a taste of that."

"Shut the fuck up!" Troy snapped. "I don't want to ever hear you talk about her like that again."

"I see that you still have the hots for Ms. Rose. Aren't you a little too old for that stuff? Besides, I heard she had a boyfriend waiting for her back in New York. You might as well give up. Headley hates you."

"Hate is a passionate emotion, and the right man can work it in his favor. I've got Ms. Rose right where I want her," he replied smug.

"You're one conceited bastard," Maxwell laughed. "I don't know why I even bother hanging around you."

"You hang around me because you know I can tolerate your sense of humor more than Cole. By the way, where is he? I thought he was going with you?"

"He still at work and told me that he'll meet us at the club. So, I don't want to hear any excuses from you about going tonight. I want to see some hot women and they're all at the Tycoon Club. Let's go." Placing his drink on the table, Maxwell stood up and made his way to the door.

"I'm not saying long," Troy replied. "I've got to be ready for Headley. I never know what kind of scheme that little wildcat is going to toss my way next. I can't wait until I win our bet."

"I've heard whispers about the bet the two of you have going on. Want to tell me more?" Maxwell asked, pausing at the door to the den.

Troy grabbed his keys off the table and strolled out the door in front of Maxwell. "No, I don't think I'm going to tell you what it is just yet. I'm going to keep it a secret a little while longer."

The main reason he wasn't going to tell Maxwell about his bet was that his friend knew him too well. Maxwell would know the real reason he wanted to marry Headley, and he wasn't

ready for that particular secret to come out of the
bag.

Chapter Five

"Do you think you're ready for this? Sometimes some of the men can get a little wild, but they're basically good guys. I never have any real huge problems with any of them," Fancy said, checking her appearance in the mirror one last time.

Headley didn't know what to say. She never expected to be working in a gentleman's club when she came back home. "I think I can handle it. I'm pretty sure that I'll know most of the guys here anyway. I don't think any of them would say anything offensive to me."

"Yeah, I think you're right, but you never know," Fancy retorted. "I still can't believe you came back home. All you talked about in high school was moving to New York and making it big as a fashion designer. Was it all you thought it would be?"

Headley wanted to tell Fancy all her dreams about moving out of town had come true, but in reality, the fashion design world was a hard place to break into.

She had a few good clients that paid her well, but it wasn't the fantasy she had it thought it would be.

In reality, she had been thinking about moving back home before she got the phone call about her father. "I wasn't what I thought it would be. Don't get me wrong, I loved it there and the freedom I had, but something was missing."

"Maybe you were missing that hottie, Troy Christian. I swear that man get sexier every time I see him. He used to come in here all the time, but in the past couple of years, he's only here about twice a month."

Her mouth opened and closed a couple of times as she tried to figure out what to say. Fancy was living in a dream world. She had never thought about Troy while she was living in New York. He had been the furthest thought from her mind.

"I don't know what you're talking about," Headley said as she joined Fancy at the mirror. "Troy never entered my mind. I was having way too much fun dating all the good looking guys there."

"Sure..." Fancy snickered as she pulled her dark brown hair back into a ponytail, making her almond shaped eyes pop even more. "Remember who you're talking to. I was about the only person that knew about your crush on Troy."

"I was barely sixteen years old back then. All the girls here had a crush on Troy when he moved to town. So, don't try that with me."

Shaking her head, Fancy tied the red t-shirt underneath her breasts. The dark color made her caramel skin stand out even more and Headley knew that was the reason Fancy decided to wear that particular color. Her friend always knew how to make her looks stand out even more.

"Yeah...I admit that I did drool over him myself a few times, but that all stopped when I noticed how he would watch you. I'm still surprised that you never saw it. It wasn't like he tried to hide his interest in you."

"Troy Christian was a snob from the first moment he moved across the way from my family, and he stayed that way until the day I moved away," Headley argued.

She never imagined a guy as mature as Troy had ever taken noticed of her.

"I'm just calling it as I see it. I know if you not been jail bait, he would have been all over you like a bear to honey."

Like a bear to honey? Where in the hell did her friend come up with this stuff?

Laughing, Headley ran her fingers through her hair and adjusted her t-shirt. It was a size too small and it made her full breasts look even bigger. "Did Tommy say when my new shirt might come in? This shirt is too tight," she complained.

"I don't know. He told me he was going to order it, but he didn't say when. Besides, you look hot and the hotter you look here, the better the tips are. Now, smile and be nice. Remember most of these guys went to school with us and only the really wealthy ones like Troy and his friends get the VIP room. It's the section in the very back of the club."

Thank God, I didn't get assigned to work there tonight, Headley thought.

"I still think this is a bad idea. I haven't been in such a long time," Troy complained as a leggy brunette led him, Maxwell and Cole to the very back of the club. Tommy had reserved this spot especially for them since his grand opening.

"Stop with all the damn complaining and take a seat," Cole snapped, dropping his six feet four inch frame into the booth. "I came here to relax and drink, not to hear you complain."

"You know he's right," Maxwell agreed looking at him before he took a seat. "This is a guy's night out. Not listen to Troy bitch about his life."

"Have I ever told the two how much I hate you?" Troy laughed as he sat at end of the leather booth. "God, if we hadn't been friends for so long, I would trade the two of you in."

"Can I get you gentlemen something to drink?" the brunette asked, but her eyes were directed on him. He was used to women eyeing

59

him and he gave her a small smile. "Why don't you bring us the best whiskey you have and three shot glasses?"

"Sure thing," she smiled and then walked away with a sway to her hips.

"Now, that's a sexy woman. I wonder if she would like a little Irish in her," Cole mumbled next to him.

"Cole, calm down. The night is young and there are probably a lot more women here for you to drool over," Troy complained, leaning back against the seat.

"What crawled up your ass and died?"

"Haven't you heard?" Maxwell asked, his eyes swinging back and forth between him and Cole.

"Heard what? Did I miss something?"

"The luscious Ms. Headley Rose is back in town and she is pissed at our Troy here. She thinks he tricked her father into signing those property rights over to him for the mega money loan he borrowed."

"No shit!" Cole muttered. "How does she look?"

"Let's just say she's gotten even better with age. Her body is a work of art. If she ever looked my way, I'd be all over that. You know I've always had a sweet tooth for chocolate and dark chocolate at that."

"Enough," Troy growled. "I've warned you once about Headley. If I have to do it again, you won't like it. Keep her name off your lips Maxwell and that goes for you too Cole. I don't want either one of you making a play for her. I've got very special plans for her, and the two of you aren't going to ruin them."

"Plans....what sort of plans?" Cole inquired as the waitress came back with their drink and glasses.

Troy waited for her to place the items in front of them. "Can I get you anything else?" The double meaning was clear and he wasn't about to take the bait.

He only had one woman in mind and it wasn't the one standing in front of him.

"No...thank you, but maybe you can send a different girl back later to take our food order."

The girl blinked a couple of times at his statement like she hadn't heard him correctly while his buddies chuckled in the background. One thing he couldn't stand was when a woman offered herself up to him so freely. He liked the hunt, the thrill of the chase.

"Yes sir...Mr. Christian," the girl snapped, and then stormed out.

"God, you're in a bad mood. You didn't have to run her off like that. I wanted to get her number," Cole muttered next to him. "You need to get laid and soon. All that built up aggression isn't good for your health at your age."

"I'll be thirty-three on my next birthday. I'm not an old man. Hell, you're five years older than me Cole."

"I know I am and I'm getting laid more than you two," his friend tossed back. "That's why I'm not acting like a bear with a thorn in his paw. Just find a woman and have a good night of sex, no commitment required."

"I've gotten too mature for a one night stand. I still can't believe the two of you still do it."

"Hey, don't bring me into this conversation," Maxwell complained as he reached for the whiskey. "I just came here tonight for some liquor and fun. I don't want to get all serious. Beside Troy, you were the worst out of all three of us. For a while, you had so many different women on your arm, I had to keep a notebook to remember their names."

"That's a lie," he denied.

"No, it isn't," Cole chimed in. "You were a regular love 'em and leave 'em for years."

"This conversation is starting to piss me off. How about we change it before I leave?" Troy threatened.

"Fine," Maxwell agreed. "How's that new thoroughbred you purchased last week? I heard that he cost you a pretty penny."

Troy was amazed at how much Maxwell knew about his business and personal life, while he never knew what his best friend was up to. Maxwell had constantly stayed a mystery to him and he had been friends with the man for over seven years.

"How did you find out about that? I told the owner not to tell anyone until I got all the paperwork squared away." He despised doing business with people who couldn't keep their mouths shut. Ranching and breeding horses was a part of his life and he didn't want anyone interfering with either. Not now...not ever.

"I'll tell you about it over our meal. We need something to talk about since I can't talk about the new project in your life."

"Maxwell," his voice warned.

"Fine, I'm done for now. But one way or another, Cole and I will find out what you're up to when it comes to Headley," Maxwell promised. "You're bound to tell us sooner or later."

Maxwell better not hold his breath or he won't make it, Troy thought. His personal business with Headley was for him to know and no one else to find out about. *End of story*.

Chapter Six

Hurrying around the main dining area, Headley took the drink orders as fast as she could and brought them back to the right tables. She hadn't been a waitress since she her college years when she had taken a second job to help with her college expenses in New York. But none of the places she worked had clients like this.

Most of the men here were wealthy and probably could pay off her debts without thinking twice about it. But she wasn't them. She had to work to get what she needed. She was about to head to a table at the right side of the club when Kendall ran smack into her.

"Watch out Headley! God, I don't need this tonight," Kendall snapped as she shoved her out of her way and continued to the back.

"What's her damn problem?" She whispered to Fancy as she passed her with a food order.

"Some guy in the VIP section pissed her off. I heard her yelling at Tommy about it a few minutes ago. She wanted him to do something about it and Tommy said no. So, Kendall quit. She has always been a drama queen and I'm glad that she's gone."

"She's crazy to quit because the tips in the VIP section are unbelievable. In one night one girl made about a grand."

"You can't be serious," Headley whispered. She needed to land that golden position. With tips like that, she would have Troy off her back in no time. "Do you know who's going to replace Kendall?"

"No. I don't. But Tommy is going to have to do it fast. Those guys don't like to be kept waiting for another," Fancy replied. "Girl, I have to go and get this food delivered. Do you want to do something after our shift is over?"

Headley would love to go out, but she had to visit her father at the hospital. "I can't. I've got to visit my dad. Maybe we can do something tomorrow?"

"Cool...I'll talk to you later about doing something." Fancy flashed a dimpled grin and then she was off flirting with every guy that she passed.

Headley shook her head at her friend and then refocused her attention back to which table was her next order. She had been working steadily for about forty-five minutes when she heard her name being yelled behind her. Turning around, she saw Tommy waving at her from his office.

"Headley, I need to see you after you drop those orders off at the bar," he yelled.

"Okay, boss." She quickly finished up the last of her orders, dropped them off with the bartender, and made her way towards Tommy's office.

"What's up?" She asked coming inside the room.

"I know that you're trying to earn extra money fast, and I'm sure you heard that Kendall quit on me." Tommy began.

"Yes, I heard rumors, but I wasn't sure if it was true or not."

"Well, it is and I need someone to take her place in the VIP room and I thought about you. Are you up for it? Sometimes those guys can get a little rowdy, but it's all in good fun. However, they're very good tippers. Working up there, you'll make good money in no time."

Headley wanted to jump up and down with joy, but she kept herself calm. She didn't need to act like a fool in front of Tommy. She could get all excited in the bathroom later.

"Are you sure about picking me? I know that Fancy wanted to take her place." Headley wanted and needed the money. However, she didn't want to push her friend out of the way to get it.

"Don't worry. I'm going to send Fancy up there with you. She knows more about taking the food orders than you, so she can help you out. Just tell her about it and then head on up there. I'm sure those guys are ready to order something to eat by now."

"Sure thing and thanks again for doing this. You don't know how much this money is going to help me out."

"Not a problem," Tommy smiled.

Headley gave Tommy a quick goodbye and then rushed from the room in search of Fancy. She sent up a silent prayer in hopes that she'd make enough tonight to make a small dent in the money Troy was complaining about.

The sooner she placed thousands of miles between them, the better chance she had on not acting out her deepest desires. Troy was a sinful fantasy that she wanted no part of. He could seduce her into his bed and she wouldn't think twice about following him there.

Troy reclined back in the booth and half-heartedly listened as Maxwell and Cole talked about business, women and money. None of it really interested him enough to make him join in as he had in the past, because his mind was totally focused on the present and Headley.

He had called her at her father's house several times before he finally decided to leave with Maxwell, but there was no answer. She had better not be out doing something she shouldn't be doing to get money. He had already given her a way out but she turned him down.

It still stung that Headley thought she was too good to accept his marriage proposal, but in the end, she would agree.

His memories of her from the past were so pure and clear. Headley had a way of carrying herself that drew his attention no matter what the time of day. At night, his cock would get so hard just thinking about having her in his bed, but he never acted on his feelings.

At that time, Headley had still been in high school and it wouldn't have been proper, so he vowed to wait until she graduated and then approach her about a relationship. However, all of his plans blew up in his face when she moved away.

The thought of visiting Headley in New York crossed his mind several times, but he never acted on it. He wasn't sure of how she would react to finding him standing outside of her dorm room, and honestly, a part of him didn't want to find her with another guy.

Troy had secretly wondered if Headley had known how he felt about her and purposely moved away from him. She always got so jumpy when he came within twenty feet of her.

Furthermore, she used her friends like a protective barrier between them.

He could count on one hand all the times he was able to get her alone, and then it was only for a few minutes.

His need to make love to Headley had built up so much over the years that he dreamt about making love to her night after night. Sometimes his desires came to him at work.

After sleeping with endless women, he thought he had the desire under control until he finally realized none of those women were giving him what he truly wanted. That was when he stopped playing games with them.

He had only wanted one woman for the past ten years of his life. He never thought he would get her. But luck was on his side and Headley was home. Come hell or high water, she was going to be his.

When Troy thought he smelled the light scent of her perfume, he knew that he was slowly losing his mind over Headley. Of course, that was impossible since she was nowhere near him.

"Excuse me, we're here to take your order," a soft, raspy voice whispered next to him.

Looking to the side, he only took a quick glance at the pretty waitress because the other waitress was who drew his instant attention. "What are you doing here?"

"What does it look like I'm doing, Mr. Christian? I'm working." Headley snapped, glaring at him. "I need to get a job so I can pay you back."

"I demand that you quit!" He growled, jumping up from his seat and moving around the other waitress.

Troy couldn't take his eyes off of the t-shirt, which hugged Headley's perfect breasts or the jeans which showed off her flawless body. She would have the money she owed him working here in no time. No...this wasn't happening to him.

"You can't tell me what to do, Troy."

"Headley, don't test me." He threatened as he stalked closer to her. He didn't give a damn that there were other people in the room. He would carry her out of here.

Other men wouldn't be looking at his woman in that outfit. It showed way too much and making his cock harder and harder by the minute. Without a doubt, Maxwell was getting off looking at all of Headley's exposed skin.

"I'm not trying to test you, but you have no right to tell me what to do," Headley tossed back.

"I've every right."

A wrinkle formed in the middle of her forehead as Headley frowned at him. "Are you drunk or something? You don't have any rights over me."

"You're mine and I won't have other men lusting after you in that barely there outfit."

Shaking her head, Headley stepped around him and laughed. "You've definitely had too much to drink because I've never been *yours* and I never will be."

Troy's hand shot out and wrapped around Headley's arm before she took ten steps away from him. "Go and tell Tommy you're quitting. I'm not going to ask you again."

Headley jerked her arm away from him as her dark eyes flashed with anger. "You don't control me. I'm not one of these girls here trying to get your attention."

"Headley...maybe you should just let it go," Fancy chimed in next to her. "You don't want to lose this job."

"Why don't you listen to your friend?" Troy couldn't let Headley work here, because if she did, he would be here every night standing guard over her. He wouldn't let another man's hands anywhere near her body.

"Fancy....needs to stay out of our conversation. This is between you and me. I've told you NO and that is the end of it. Now go away."

Something intense flared through Troy at the way Headley was standing up to him. He tried to fight the overwhelming need to jerk her into his arms and kiss her senseless, but he failed. He had to have a taste of her or he was going to lose his mind.

Without giving her any warning, he grabbed her by the waist and tossed her over his shoulder, storming out of the VIP room. "I told you not to challenge me and you just don't listen."

"Put me down!" Headley screamed as her small fists pounded him in the middle of his back. "You're embarrassing me."

"Stop that," Troy uttered smacking Headley on her denim-clad bottom. He tried not to be carried away by how good her tight ass felt underneath his hand. He'd make sure that he'd explore that later.

He kept walking until he reached Tommy's office where he didn't bother to knock, but walked right on in. A stunned Tommy stared at them from his position behind his desk. "Leave now. I need to speak to Headley alone."

"Is everything okay?" Tommy inquired standing up.

"No...everything isn't okay," Headley yelled, squirming around on his shoulder. "I'm being manhandled by Troy and I want him to put me down."

Troy didn't hesitate at all before giving Headley's tight ass another loud smack. "We're having a lover's spat. I brought her in here so we can talk. She's so fiery that I didn't want the entire club listening to us."

"Hmmm...okay. I'll go down to the basement and check the liquor. I was going to do it later, but now is as good a time as any." Tommy came around the desk, quickly dashing past Troy and a thrashing Headley.

A few seconds later, the door closed softly behind him.

He didn't get a chance to put Headley down before she was beating him on the back again.

"Haven't I told you to stop doing that?" he chuckled as he slipped her down the front of his body.

A shiver ran through him as her soft breasts brushed over his chest. It had been such a long time since he'd wanted to lose himself in a woman's body.

Holding Headley close to him, he backed them up until her back touched the desk behind them.

"You smell so good," he whispered burying his nose below her ear. "I could just eat you up." Nipping at her neck, Troy cupped Headley's ass in his hands and held her against him. "Why don't we just stop all of this fighting and get down to the good stuff?"

"Troy, you aren't going to seduce me into giving in to you," Headley moaned near his ear. "I'll fight you every step of the way."

"That's such a waste of energy. I know we can find a better way for you to get rid of it. With the built up sexual tension we have, we'll be explosive together. Hell...the fire alarm will go off when we finally give in."

"You're wrong," she denied with a shake of her head. "I don't want you."

Inching back, Troy stared at Headley while she fought to keep her body under control. Yet he could see how hard her nipples were through the thin t-shirt.

Reaching out, he ran his hand slowly down the front of her shirt pausing long enough to give each nipple a firm pinch.

Headley gasped but didn't tell him to stop. Instead she drew her full bottom lip between her teeth and waited.

He slowly ran his fingers over her bare stomach almost getting lost in the silkiness of it.

"Are you sure that you want to get into another bet with me? I'm already going to win this bet. Do you really want to get into another with me?"

He was ready to prove that there was more than a strong sexual pull between them. His whole being seemed to be waiting for her response. All he needed was the word, and Headley would be screaming his name.

"You're a smug something, aren't you?" Headley asked running her hand down the middle of his chest. "How do you know I'm not faking my need for you?"

His lips recaptured her, more demanding this time. Parting her lips, he thrust his tongue inside and devoured its softness. He had to prove he was the only man for her. A low growl erupted from his throat when Headley's arms wrapped around his neck and her hips grounded against his.

Tearing his mouth away, he nibbled a path down her neck while his hands eased between them and he unbuttoned her pants. Slipping a hand inside, he worked two fingers into her wetness.

"Fuck…you're so damn tight! Will your hold my cock this snug when I finally get inside of you?"

"Oh, I really do hate you," she panted dropping her head to his shoulder.

"Oh really," Troy taunted as he wiggling a third finger inside Headley's warm dampness. Her body sucked him in without a problem. "Double fuck…I'm going to lose my mind if I don't get to make love to you and soon."

Low mewling sounds erupted from Headley as her hips worked to keep up with his fingers. "You play so unfair," she moaned as her teeth nibbled at his earlobe.

"Darling, I never play fair when it comes to something I want, and I want you." Troy didn't mind that his erection was about to spilt the front of his slacks, because Headley was finally in his arms giving in to the desire for him. All he needed was a few more seconds and she would cum all over his fingers. Just the thought of it made his cock grow another inch.

"Come on baby....cum for me. I want to pull my fingers out of you and taste your sweetness. Will it be better than honey? Or will I have to undress you and sample you again and again until I come up for the perfect name to describe your unique favor?"

"Oh....God, stop," she whimpered as her short nails dug into his forearm. The pain only heightened his sense of arousal.

Using his free hand, Troy cupped Healey's face and made her look at him. "Say you'll marry me. You can't get the money in time. I can make you feel this good all year long."

Dark sienna eyes clouded with passion stared at him. He could see that Headley was fighting a battle within herself. Would she say yes or would her stubborn side win over?

He saw the exact moment when the latter occurred. Sadness replaced the passion in her eyes and a sad smile tugged at the corners of her lush mouth.

"Troy...I can't" She whispered as she pulled his hand from her pants. "I've got to do this for my father."

"What about you? Shouldn't you have some time for yourself? If you're married to me Douglas' debt will be gone."

"Don't you understand that I don't want you to win the bet? I've got to prove I can do this. That's how my dad got into this problem. He didn't wait it out long enough. I know deep down I can get this money back to you, even if it means working another job."

A muscle worked in Troy's jaw as he watched Headley fix her clothes. He hated how she didn't want to lean on him for help. It didn't matter that he was the one who caused her to be in this situation in the first place.

"Tell me the truth. You want to win because the thought of being married to me sickens you, doesn't it? You haven't changed at all. You avoided me when you were younger, and you're still doing it."

Folding her arms underneath her breasts, Headley cocked her head and stared at him. "You aren't making any sense. I never avoided you when I was younger. God, you were older than me. We hung out with different crowds. You were like the dark haired God every girl in town dreamt about. I'm sure you had plenty of attention without me adding to your adoring fan club."

"What if I told you I only wanted one girl to be in my fan club?"

"I would say it would have been anyone but me," Headley sighed. "Look...I've got to get back to work before I lose this job. I'll see you later to discuss a payment plan."

Troy stood still as Headley strolled past him and went out the door. This time he let her leave because he saw their conversation was over. However, he wasn't giving up. Headley was going to be his, whether she realized it or not.

Chapter Seven

The water pounded around her in the shower as Headley tried working the stiffness out of her back and shoulders. She had forgotten how waiting tables could take a lot out of her body.

Why aren't you being honest with yourself? Waiting tables tonight isn't what made your body sore and stiff. Making out with Troy on top of Tommy's desk is what tore up your body. He was all over you and you did nothing to stop it.

How was she supposed to pay off this dumb ass debt and leave Paris if her need for Troy was growing deeper and deeper with each passing moment? She couldn't give in to it.

He was just trying to seduce her into his bed. He wasn't serious about marrying her. Troy owned most of the property in this town. Why would he want to settle down with her?

No, he was up to something, and tomorrow when she had her weekly meeting with him, she would find out what it was.

Turning off the shower, she stepped out to wrap a towel around herself then strolled into her bedroom. She quickly dried her body and climbed into bed. Headley thought that she would be up tossing and turning thinking about Troy, but as soon as her head hit the pillow, she was sound asleep.

All Troy could think about was what happened with Headley at the club, and he was very pleased with the way things were going. She responded to him with such zeal last night that there was no way she wasn't attracted to him.

They were going to burn up the sheets when she finally gave in to him. All he had to do was just keep at it and Headley would finally be his after all of these years.

It was beyond a shock seeing her last night in one of those skimpy outfits. He wanted her to quit her job at the club, but she wasn't about to do that. So, he had to take matters into his own hands.

Now, after the talk he just had with Tommy, Headley wouldn't be coming in to work tonight or any other night for that matter. He had to give her credit. Headley was smart. With a job at the Tycoon's club, she might have come really close to paying off the bet. But he had made sure that wouldn't be a possibility.

Nope. Headley was going to be his wife in a matter of weeks and he couldn't wait. He was finally going to get the upper hand after all of these years.

She never knew how he'd gone to her father to ask if he could date her once she turned eighteen. Douglas had laughed in his face and tossed him out of their house.

It had been a blow to his ego, but he that didn't make him give up hope that one day Headley would see him as a man she could love. All of his dreams died when he watched her get on that bus and leave town.

Headley and Douglas were both clueless to the fact that he had followed them to the bus station. He had hidden in the shadows watching them say good-bye to each other. It took all of his willpower not to beg her not to leave.

Nevertheless, he had made a promise to himself that day. He would find a way to get back at both of them and now his time had finally come.

What better revenge could he have than being married to Headley?

She constantly thought she was better than he. He was not about to believe she never knew how he felt. How could she not? He wore his heart on his sleeve when it came to her.

Every time she turned around when they were younger, he was there. Did she truly think all of those meetings were accidental?

For years after she left home, all he thought about was how it would have been if Douglas hadn't kicked him out of the house that day. Headley's father never gave him a chance to plead his case. He never thought he would get the opportunity to get back at the Rose family until that one perfect day Douglas came begging for help.

He was taken back by how much money the old man had wasted on bad investments, drinking and gambling. Maybe he had overcharged him a bit when it came to the interest, but it had felt good to have the great Douglas Rose begging for help.

However, he never wanted the old man to have a heart attack and end up in the hospital.

After all, Douglas was the only parent Headley had left, and he knew that she would be back in town after the news got to her. So, that's why he had made the phone call to her job.

She didn't know he was the one who had tracked her down and she never would. Headley's place was here in Paris with him, not the hustle and bustle of fast-paced New York City. She wasn't made for that lifestyle.

"I'm not going to lose her for a second time," he swore softly.

A slight noise outside his office drew Troy's attention away from his inner thoughts. The sound of Heather, his secretary, yelling at someone made him jump up from his seat and hurry around his desk.

He was half-way to his office door when Headley barged through looking gorgeous in all white.

"Hello, Headley. Is there something I can do for you?" Troy already knew why Headley was here, but he wanted to hear the words from her mouth.

"I want you to call Tommy and tell him to give me my job back," Headley snapped, slamming the door behind her in Heather's shocked face. "I need that job and I want it back."

"I have no say in who Tommy fires and hires," he replied coming back across the room and retaking his seat. "Maybe you didn't do a good job last night and that's the reason he let you go."

"That's the same crap Tommy tried to feed me," Headley huffed.

"I love how sexy you are when you get upset. Your right eyebrow does this little twitch and your breasts start to heave." Troy commented glancing down at Headley's white pullover top, then back up to her eyes. "Your fire makes me want to ravish you in the middle of my office."

"Have you lost your mind? I'm here because I want answers and you're talking about having sex."

"Making love," he corrected quickly. As long as he had waited to get Headley into his bed, having sex was the last thing on his mind. He wanted to make love all night long and early into the morning.

"Same difference," she uttered with a wave of her hand.

"No, there's a big difference, darling." Troy replied standing up.

He moved around his desk and back towards Headley, stopping mere inches from her body.

"Greedy men have sex because they want to satisfy their own need. I'm not a greedy man. I'm going to make love to you because I want to *enjoy* every perfect inch of your body. From those plump lips that I want to suck, down to those amazing legs that will be wrapped around my waist while I erupted inside your welcoming body."

He watched as all the anger disappeared from Headley's body as his words settled in and a small smile of wonder touched her lips. She was totally unaware of the breathtaking picture she made when she smiled at him.

"You're very confident in your abilities when it comes to me," she mused. "This could be all talk for all I know."

"Give me a few minutes to get things settled here, and I'll take you back to my place. I'll prove everything I just told you," he promised in a low voice.

"It's not going to happen. I'm going to see Tommy about my job and if that doesn't work, I've got one last ace up my sleeve. I still have two weeks to get your money to you."

Tommy wasn't going to give Headley her job back. Just like he had made sure, no one else in town would give her one. He had made sure all the cards were stacked in his favor. Still, this ace thing had him worried.

"Headley, don't do anything you can't get out of, just to beat me."

"A bet is a bet and I'm in it to win it. I've one last person in mind to ask for the rest of the money. I know he can help me."

His teeth clenched in anger. He was furious! Headley was eager to run to another man in order to beat him, but he wasn't good enough for her. It was like the past all over again. She still thought she was too good for him. He swallowed hard, trying not to reveal his anger.

"You aren't going to use another man's money to pay off your father's debt to me. The only way you're going to get out of this is by marrying me."

Headley glowered at him. "You aren't making any sense. I was going to give you money from Tommy. So, what difference does it make it if get it from a man you don't know?"

"I won't take money from one of your lovers in New York. Don't even think about contacting him," Troy snapped as jealousy ate him up.

"This may be news to you, Troy, but a man and woman can be friends without sleeping together. Avant has money and he'll loan it to me. I can pay him back over time."

Headley was desperately trying to find a way out of this mess. She was such an idiot for making the bet in the first damn place. She should have just asked for a payment plan and Troy might have agreed. No...she had to go and challenge him with a bet, of all things.

Troy's competitive side was one of the things she found so sexy about him.

At every picnic or outdoor activity, he always played to win. She would pretend not to watch him when she was younger, but the way the sun shined off his dark hair made her stomach clench.

Back then, he had only been in his twenties, but he already had the body of man. A flat washboard stomach and muscles that bulged in places she had never seen before.

All she thought about was kissing him, or better yet, having him crawl through her window at night and make love to her. However, none of her fantasies ever came true.

She was living in such a dream world that the night she had left town, she had imagined seeing Troy hiding in the shadows looking at her.

But of course that hadn't been real. Troy was mature beyond his years back then, and never paid her a second glance until the day her mother died.

Troy's reaction to her borrowing the money from Avant surprised her. She would think he would be overjoyed about getting his money back and her out of his life.

The quicker he got the money deposited into her account, the sooner she could be back on a plane headed back home.

"I know that, but I don't believe there's a man out there who only wants to be friends with you. If by some slim chance there is, he has to be crazy or gay."

"Avant isn't crazy or gay. We went out on a few dates, but things didn't work out. We decided to be friends instead."

"Darling, there's something wrong with him if he doesn't want you. Maybe he just doesn't know it yet," Troy's warm voice replied.

His tone both aroused and infuriated her. Why did she have to be attracted to the *one* man on the planet who only wanted sex from her and nothing else?

Troy's marriage proposal had no merit behind it. He would never go through with it. She was furious at her weakness for him.

"Stop that," she whispered.

"Stop what?" Troy said the words quietly, but his voice held a sexual undertone to it. "Can't I tell a beautiful woman that I want and need her? I thought you would be used to it by now."

"Listen, I'm not going down this road with you. I can't stand here and listen to this. I need to visit my father at the hospital and see what I can do about finding another job," Headley replied, stepping back from Troy.

"Do you want me to come to the hospital with you?"

Headley didn't know what shocked her more, Troy's offer or the urge to say yes. He was getting under her skin. She had to put some distance between them.

"No, I can go by myself, but thanks for the offer." She turned to leave but Troy's voice stopped her.

"Headley wait," he uttered. "I can go with you. I know it must be hard for you to see your father like that. Can't we just put our differences to the side for an hour and let me be there for you?"

Glancing over her shoulder, she was about to tell Troy no again until she saw the sincerity on his face. He honestly looked like he wanted to be there for her. It touched a place in her heart that she wanted to keep hidden from the handsome man behind her.

"Okay...I would like for you to come," she finally agreed.

"Wonderful," he smiled coming towards her. "We can take my car and I'll bring you back here afterwards."

Troy escorted her out the door and paused in front of his secretary's desk. "Heather, I'll be gone for a couple of hours. If someone needs me, just take a message and I'll get back to them later."

"Are you going somewhere with Ms. Rose?" Heather asked, looking at her, then back at Troy.

Headley had the feeling that Heather was a little jealous that Troy was leaving with her.

"Yes....I am," Troy answered as he led her away towards the elevators.

She stood quietly beside Troy while they waited for the elevators to come. A small part of her wondered if Troy knew how he made women fall for him.

He truly acted like he never saw the jealousy in Heather's eyes when she looked at them. Or was it a woman scorned by the fact that man who had been involved with her was with another woman?

"I think Heather was upset by the fact that you're leaving with me."

Dark blue eyes glanced down at her as the elevator doors opened. Troy waved her in ahead of him and then followed her in. He didn't say anything until the door closed and he punched the button for the parking lot.

"What are you talking about? Heather doesn't care if I'm going with you. We don't have that kind of relationship. She's my employee and nothing else," he replied.

"Are you sure that she doesn't want anything more? You're an attractive man and she looked at you like she hoped something more would happen."

"Nothing is going to happen with her. She isn't my type."

Men, she thought. They always had a *type*.

"Aren't you going to tell me more? What kind of women gets the great Troy Christian all hot and bothered?" She would love to hear that he was only looking for one woman and that woman was her, but that was never going to happen.

Sure, she was nice-looking to a certain point. Yet, she was never the type Troy would date.

"I want a woman who can make me laugh, but knows how to stand up for herself when the time calls for it. I don't need someone who is always at my beck and call. Independence is a good thing, but not to the point where she wants to wear the pants. I'm the man, and I want it to stay that away."

"Okay...you've told me about her personality, but what are you looking for when it comes to looks? Because I thought Heather's dark brown hair and green eyes would have you doing a double-take."

The sound of the elevator as it moved from the sixteenth floor down to the basement was the only sound in the area as Troy watched her from the corner of his eye. Headley was getting a little nervous at the silence. Whenever Troy got this quiet, it meant he was up to something.

"It's hard for me to envision another woman when I have only wanted one woman for most of my life," he commented, facing her. "She's drop-dead gorgeous and anytime I try to make her believe I'm serious about her, she blows me off."

"My woman has Hershey's kiss chocolate skin and it makes me want to run my fingers all over it. Her soft brown eyes continuously give me the impression that she can see into my soul every time she looks at me. She has the most perfect body, I have ever seen in my life. Her breasts and hips are what dreams are made of," he continued in a low voice.

"A night doesn't go by that I don't dream about her lying in bed next to me, or me waking her up with soft kisses as I work my way down her body. Sometimes I wake up with my cock is so hard that I can't leave the bed until I relieve the ache over and over. Do you know how unfeeling it is for me to be alone, taking care of my own needs when I would rather be wrapped inside your tight little body?"

Headley took a deep breath and closed her eyes as a pool of moisture soaked her panties. Why did Troy have to say these things to her? Lord...he was trying to make her lose control when it came to him.

Her eyes popped open when she felt a hand slip between her legs and stoke the inside of her thigh. "What are you doing?" she squeaked as she grabbed Troy's thick wrist.

"Nothing," Troy whispered as his tongue licked the corner of her mouth. "I just wanted to touch you. Don't you want me to touch you?" He asked, shaking off her light grip. "We both know that I can make you feel so good."

There was a maddening hint of arrogance about him that should make her hate Troy, but it only turned her on even more. He was so disturbing to her in every sense of the word.

For years, she had dreamed of being crushed in his embrace and her feelings for him were intensifying.

"God...you know that I do, but we...I can't," she moaned, shoving Troy away from her. "It wouldn't turn out good in the end. We are so incompatible."

Stepping back, Troy folded his arms across his chest displaying his muscles through his shirt. "We're a perfect match. All you have to do is open your eyes and see what's right in front of you."

The elevator doors opening stopped Headley from answering, and she hurried out with

Troy behind her. "Let's go and see my father. I can't talk to you about this anymore."

She sent up a silent prayer for her rescue once again from giving in to her deepest desires. Troy was so close at wearing her down and he didn't even know it.

"Headley, we aren't done with this. I've waited for too long to give you up now," Troy uttered behind her, but she kept going as if she never heard him say a word.

Chapter Eight

Relaxing against the wall, Troy blocked out the smell of floor cleaner and day old coffee as he watched Healey at her father's bedside.

He admired how strong she was trying to be, however he could see that the woman he was in love with was hurting. Why didn't he just tell her to forget about the money and let her go? It wasn't doing either of them any good going back and forth like they were.

She was taking so much onto her small shoulders with Douglas' money problems, trying to find a way to pay him back and now fighting not to fall into his bed at any second. Headley thought she was doing a good job at hiding her feelings for him, but he knew she wanted him.

He fought down the urge to wrap her up in his arms, to promise that everything would be okay, but he couldn't do it. Douglas wasn't looking too good to him. His breathing was shallow, and before they came in, the nurse told them, he had had a bad night.

Headley wouldn't be able to handle it if her father died. He remembered how hard she took it when her mother and baby brother died. She put on a strong show at the funerals, but he had seen the tears glistening in her brown eyes.

 Right then, he almost told her how he felt, but decided it wasn't the correct time. She would have been shocked by his confession.

"Daddy, can you hear me? It's me, Headley. I'm here with you," she whispered, holding her father's hand.

His heart clenched in his chest at the sight of her using her free hand to brush away her tears. There was nothing he could do to help Headley with this. Maybe if he had found Douglas sooner, he wouldn't be in this bed.

Was he really the one to blame for the heart attack? Douglas had lost a lot of his workers because he didn't have the money to pay them. That was the reason he was out repairing the fence instead of someone else. Could Headley really see him for the man that he was and not the man who had put her father in this room?

"Daddy, I just want you to know that I'm here for you and I'm not going to leave until you get better."

Troy couldn't take it anymore. The pain in Headley's voice was about to break him and make him say something that he shouldn't. He couldn't let Headley out of the bet because that was the only way he would get his ring on her finger.

The thought barely crossed his mind before another one followed. He had to get out of here to be alone with his thoughts for a few minutes.

Moving away from his spot, he made his way across the room and leaned down to whisper in Headley's ear. "Darling, I'm going into the hallway so you can have some private time with your father."

"Okay," Headley answered without looking at him.

Troy gave Headley's shoulder a quick squeeze before he left the room closing the door quietly behind him.

Outside in the hallway, he watched the nurses as they walked past him and checked on other patients.

The harder he tried to ignore the truth, the more it persisted. He was heads over heels in love with Headley. How much longer could he keep doing this before he blurted out the truth?

"I still can't believe Troy took you to the hospital to see your father," Fancy said, placing the clean glasses on a shelf. "I thought the two of you weren't even friends."

"Troy is a mystery that I can't figure out," Headley answered, playing with a peanut on the bar. "I know he was the one who told Tommy to fire me and then he turns around and does something nice. I'm at a total loss when it comes to him."

"Well... you know what I think," Fancy said, facing her. "I think he likes you and you're being blind to it on purpose."

Headley groaned under her breath. "Don't start that again. I'm not interested in finding a man, and if I was, Troy Christian isn't even what I'm looking for."

"Now...I know you're just a damn liar. Troy Christian is plain lip-licking magnificent." Fancy looked around making sure they were alone in the club before she leaned across the bar. "I bet his dick is at least nine inches long. Have you noticed how he walks? Only a man with a big package swaggers like that."

"FANCY!" She snapped, and then hit her friend on the arm. "You can't talk about a guy like that." However, she had noticed the enormous bulge inside Troy's pants. Hell, it was hard to miss.

"It's past time you got a grip and had a little fun. You're always so serious. Live a little and go after him. I know he wouldn't turn you down, like some men I know."

Fancy wasn't able to let that hang in the air between them. Was there a man her friend wanted and couldn't get? She wanted details. "Okay, spill it. Who do you have your eye on? Is it Tommy?"

"Tommy, my boss," Fancy sputtered. "No, I don't want Tommy. God... I've seen him eat glue. I don't think so."

Headley shook her head and wondered about Fancy. "Tommy ate glue in the second grade. I don't think he has done it lately," she sighed. "He's nice. I think the two of you would make a very cute couple."

"Nope, Tommy isn't the man I want."

"I'm not going to stop asking until you tell me," Headley said. "Do I know him?"

Fancy started wiping off the bar's surface like she hadn't heard a word that she said, but Headley knew her friend had heard every word. What guy out there didn't want Fancy? She was almost model perfect, despite being almost four inches too short for the industry. However, her personality and spunk made up for it.

"Answer me."

"It doesn't matter because he has turned me down enough times for me to leave it alone," Fancy sighed.

"I'm not going to leave this alone. You keep getting in my face about Troy and I'm going to return the favor. If I guess right, will you tell me then?" Headley wasn't about to give up on this. She may not be able to get Troy, but she would help Fancy get her dream man.

As Fancy opened her mouth to answer, the club's door opened and the towering frame of Maxwell Reed walked in, looking very sexy in a cream colored Stetson, snug blue jeans and a checkered shirt.

Headley noticed how Fancy couldn't take her off Troy's friend. She secretly wondered if this the guy Fancy was talking about earlier. Surely not. Maxwell had been a bachelor for as long as she could remember. He had already graduated from college and was working at his father's business when she left town. Maxwell was even older than Troy.

She had spoken to him a few times in New York at a couple of plays, and the women he was with never looked like Fancy.

"Headley, what are you doing here?" Maxwell asked, joining her at the bar. "I thought Troy told me you didn't work here anymore."

Headley frowned as a pair of moss green eyes studied her. "I see the good news traveled fast. See... I knew he got me fired just to win this damn bet."

A deep chuckle set her nerves on end. "I know nothing about that. I'm just surprised to find you here at ten o'clock in the morning."

"I came here to see Fancy. You know she works here, don't you?" She saw Fancy stiffen from the corner of her eye and wondered how much, her friend had flirted with Maxwell before.

Maxwell's eyes swung away from her over to Fancy who acted like she was rooted to the spot. A tornado couldn't have moved her stiff frame. "Yes, I know who Ms. Shayne is," he answered in a tone that was coolly disapproving. "I was surprised to find out the two of you were friends."

"Why would you say that?" She asked in a voice that barely hid her temper. How dare he insult Fancy with her standing right there.

"Ms. Shayne isn't anything like you. It would be like comparing day and night when it comes to the two of you. She's very....I'm not quite sure of the word I'm looking for..."

Headley was numb with increasing rage and shock at how Maxwell was treating Fancy. He may not like her, but that was no reason to be insulting. "Mr. Reed, Fancy is my friend, and I would appreciate if you were more respectful to her."

Looking back at her, Maxwell's eyebrows shot up under his hat. "I wasn't trying to insult Fancy at all. She's a very sweet girl with an outgoing personality. If I was rude to your friend, I apologize."

"How about you say that to Fancy instead of me?"

"No...that's okay Headley," Fancy said finally cutting into the conversation. "Mr. Reed didn't mean any harm."

She suppressed her anger under the appearance of indifference. If Fancy wanted to act like Maxwell's words hadn't hurt her feelings, then she could. Nevertheless, she wasn't going to stay any longer.

"Fine, I'm leaving. I've got to find Troy anyway. We have a few things that we need to discuss. Do you know where he is?" She asked Maxwell as she got off the barstool.

"I just let him at home. I think he was working from there today. I know that he'll be more than happy if you stopped by for a visit."

"Great. I hope you're right. We need to discuss a few things," Headley commented, then looked back at Fancy. "I'll be home later tonight. Why don't you stop by and we can go out to eat? I haven't had much time to hear what's going on in your life."

"I wish I could, but I can't," Fancy said. "I start my other job tonight and it's from eleven to seven in the morning. Can I get a rain check?"

Headley was dying to ask Fancy why she needed another job with the money Tommy was paying her at the Tycoon's Club, but she didn't in front of Maxwell.

He was pretending like he wasn't playing attention to their conversation, yet he was. It almost seemed like he was more interested in Fancy that she had first thought.

"Fine, I'll call you later and see when we can do it. Wish me luck with Troy. You know how he can be."

"Good luck and remember what we talked about earlier," Fancy grinned, then winked.

"Yeah...and you stay out of trouble," she laughed and then glanced at Maxwell. "Have a nice day Maxwell and stop being so mean to Fancy. She's so sweet."

"I never said Ms. Shayne wasn't. Have a nice meeting with Troy," his voice answered in a deep drawl.

Headley waved good-bye to the two people in the room and hurried out the door wondering how she was going to approach Troy about her new idea about the bet. She hoped that he was in a good mood and agreed to her idea.

Chapter Nine

The muscles in his body burned as his arms cut through the water, but he didn't care. He was going to finish this last lap in the pool. This was the only thing that gave his body relief anytime his thoughts ran towards Headley.

He couldn't believe how seeing her with her father yesterday bothered him. He wasn't supposed to be feeling like this. All he could think about was wrapping her up in his arms and promising to take all the pain away.

However, Headley was so strong that she probably would have pushed him away saying she didn't need or want his help.

How did things get so complicated between the two of them? All he ever wanted was for

Headley to be in his life and now she was, but it wasn't like he imagined.

Sure, they had stolen kisses here and there. He felt her attraction to him, but he deserved more than a forced sexual attraction.

A part of his was starting to realize that Headley may not be the woman for him and that cut at him deep. She was so perfect for him, and yet she couldn't see right what was in front of her face.

Swimming to the side of the pool, Troy came to the surface and brushed his hair out of his face. He wiped the water from his eyes and looked right at Headley sitting in a chair staring at him.

His heart jumped in his chest at the unexpected sight of her. "What are you doing here?"

"We need to talk about the bet," Headley answered.

A sick feeling came to the pit of his stomach. Had Healey found a way to get the money to him or was she here trying to back out? "What do you want to talk about? I'm not backing down on my end of the bet."

"I never thought you would," she replied. "Can you get out of the pool so we can discuss something?"

"Darling, I don't think that would be a good idea."

"Why not?" She asked.

"Just trust me. You don't want me to get out of the pool in front of you. How about you go inside and wait for me in the living room? I'll meet you in there in about thirty minutes."

"Troy, I've had a long morning and I don't have time to play games with you. Can you please get out of the pool and talk to me?"

"Headley, remember I warned you," Troy said before he lifted his body out of the water.

"You're naked," Headley gasped as her eyes zoned on his growing erection.

Headley couldn't take her eyes off of Troy's sculptured body. It looked like it had been made by the finest Gods in the world. Thick muscles covered his arms, making them look ultra strong and capable of never letting her go.

Her eyes moved down to the well-defined six pack that looked as if Troy spent hours in the gym to get. They made her want to drag her tongue across them to see if they tasted as good as they looked.

Dropping her eyes down, she noticed how cut his thighs were and how there wasn't an ounce of fat on his entire body. She tried not to think about what Fancy said, but it kept coming back to her. However, her curiosity got the best of her and her eyes moved to take a look.

Troy's cock was perfect. Its head was beautifully sculpted, the length and width made her jaw drop open.

Double Damn! His cock was so thick that she wondered if just the head would even fit inside of her body. Of all the times she had wondered what Troy looked like naked, none of her imaginings had ever came close to how amazing he was.

There wasn't a tan line on his perfectly tanned skin. It almost made her wonder if he sunbathed in the nude or if it was natural.

"Are you enjoying what you're seeing?" Troy asked as his erection grew another inch.

"I'm sorry," she apologized. "I didn't mean to stare at you. I can leave."

Headley started to get up as Troy quickly closed the distance between them and blocked her body in with his.

"Why are you running away? I don't care if you see me naked and hard. I've never lied about how much I want you. Do you want to touch me?" Taking her hand, Troy placed it in the middle of his chest.

She could barely contain her gasp of excitement at the feel of his warm skin under her palm. "You're so hard. I can't believe it," she whispered.

Her fingers traced the lines of Troy's chest all the way down to his flat stomach, but stopped before she got to the best part of him. This had to stop before they both got carried away.

"I can't do this," she moaned dropping her hand. "I've got to leave."

Before she could move a step, Troy grabbed her by the shoulder and yanked her to his body.

"I'm tired of you always running out on me when things get too hot. Aren't you ready to give in to what you feel is going on between us. I can't do it all. You have to meet me halfway unless you're saying you don't want me. If you don't, let me know now and I'll leave you alone."

"I'll wipe out your father's debt and you can run back to New York and hide like you've been doing for the past ten years of your life. So let me know now, because I'm just about fed up with all this hot and cold shit you're doing to me. I want you. I've wanted you for years, and now it's up to you. I'm not going to do it anymore."

Damn it! Troy was right. She had been telling him that she didn't want him but he had pushed and pushed until she had to admit to herself that she truly did want him. Hell, she wanted him more now than she did when she was a teenager.

She was running from so many things when it came to him. She was tired of living for everyone else. For once in her life, she wanted to just to live in the moment and today was going to be that day.

Standing on tiptoe, she touched her lips to his. "Troy, I've been running from you and I don't want to do that anymore," she breathed against his firm mouth. "I want to stay here with you. I'm not going to worry about tomorrow."

She tried not to flinch as Troy's grip tightened on her waist. "Are you sure about this? I don't want you to have any regrets later on."

"I'm sure," Headley whispered before sliding her hands through Troy's thick hair and kissing him completely.

Chapter Ten

Go slow...Don't rush this. I've waited too long for this moment. Troy kept telling himself that over and over as he laid Headley down on the patio chair behind them. The softness of her breasts pressing into his chest made his cock twitch.

"Say it again," he whispered as he untied the belt from her cobalt dress. Pushing the fabric away, he stared at her breasts in the matching bra. "I want to hear you tell me again."

"I want you," Headley moaned twisting her body under his. "I know this is wrong, but I can't help it. I need to have you inside of me."

Troy was trying his best to stay calm and slowly work Headley into an uncontrollable frenzy, but the sound of need in her voice sent that thought right out the window. Reclaiming her lips, he tightened his grip on her waist and yanked her body closer to his.

He couldn't think of anything more perfect than when he got the pleasure of kissing the wonderful woman in his arms. It was almost like a divine ecstasy.

Tearing her mouth away from his, Headley pressed her lips against his neck. "Please don't do this to me. I can't take it."

"Do what?" he asked trailing his fingers all over the exposed skin beneath his. He would never grow tired of learning the shape of his woman's body.

"Make me want you as much as I do. It isn't fair," Headley moaned as she started scratching his back with her short nails.

The pain felt wonderful on Troy's skin and drove him to make Headley his for the rest of their lives. If this was the only chance they got to make love, then he wanted it to be imprinted on her mind forever.

Lifting Headley up, he completely stripped her out of the dress and tossed it over his shoulder near the pool. He didn't care where it landed because she wouldn't need it for a while.

"You're so damn perfect," he uttered running his palms over Headley's breasts. Her nipples were so hard that they felt like hard pebbles to his palms. "I'm going to love making love to you for the rest of the day."

Trailing his fingers down the sides of Headley's firm breasts, Troy covered the top and nipples with tiny kisses.

The low moan from Headley's mouth pushed him to draw it further into his mouth with a slower sucking motion.

He gently eased her back down on the cushioned seat

His hand traced a path from Headley's abdomen, down her legs until he could push her silky thighs apart. He settled between them and almost lost control as the tip of his cock brushed against her warm, wet entrance.

"Oh," Headley closed her eyes and purred in the back of her throat. "You feel so good. God, I want more."

"No," he replied. "I'm not giving in to you until I'm good and ready. I've waited too damn long for this. I want you just as hungry as I am."

Headley's eyes snapped opened and she stared at him. "You're going to make me beg for sex?"

"Sweetheart, I wouldn't do anything of the sort," he smiled. "I'm just going to have you so hot that the only thing that can put out your fire is my cock in your tight little body."

Troy's mouth captured Headley's before she could say a word. He slid his tongue into her mouth in pure masculine possession. He wasn't going to let her forget who she was with.

No other man was going to stay in Headley's mind after today.

Cupping her firm ass in his hands, he pulled her closer to his body as the tip of his erection slid into her. Her body sucked at him like she had been without a man for years.

A tiny tremor went through his body as soft hands threaded into his hair. Then Headley arched her body, giving him the silent signal that she wanted him to continue with what he was doing.

"Gorgeous," he breathed against her moist mouth. "I knew you would feel like this in my arms." He tugged her bottom lip between his teeth and nibbled.

Under him, Headley wigged her butt in his hands.

Capturing her chin in his hands, he made her look at him. "Do you want more? Do you want to feel me deep inside of you?"

"You already know the answer to that," she whispered, softly.

"Tell me what you want. I don't want to make any mistakes about this. No regrets when this is over." Hell, he wasn't about to let her go after this. Headley was definitely going to marry him after this. Another man wouldn't ever see her like this and if one tried, he would kill him.

Passion coursed through his body. After all of these years, he was finally getting to live out his dream. Unless Headley had a change of mind.

No matter how crazy he was in learning what made her stunning body click, he would stop if she told me to.

"Tell me," he uttered brushing his cock against her.

A pink tongue came out and moistened Headley's lips. "Tell you what," she moaned.

"Don't play with me. My patience is barely there as it is. Tell me now."

"You... I want...no, need you."

"Doll, I thought you would never ask," Troy growled as he quickly repositioned his body so that his mouth replaced his cock.

Headley jerked at the feel of Troy's tongue licking the juices from her body. "OMIGOD," she screamed trying to squirm away from his seeking lips. "You've got to stop. I can't take it."

Ignoring her protests, he spread Headley's thighs further apart, and kept licking at the cream pouring from her body. He couldn't get enough of her. She tasted sweeter than honey and better than the richest chocolate in the world. He wasn't about to stop until he got his full.

All Troy could think about was making Headley's body love him as much as he wanted her heart to. He might have to win her body over first, but he didn't give a damn. In the end, Headley would be his for the rest of their lives and she wasn't going to be able to fight him anymore.

Keeping her thighs where he wanted them, Troy ate at Headley like a prisoner being served his last meal.

He didn't flinch when she grabbed a handful of his hair and pressed him even closer to her wet entrance. In fact, it pushed him to lick and suck even harder.

"Troy! God, don't Stop!" Her orgasms filled his mouth and he didn't stop until every last delicious drop was gone from her thrashing body.

"Oh, baby....you taste so fucking good," he moaned licking the side of Headley's legs before kissing his way back up her body. "I can't wait until I'm inside of you."

Without giving Headley a chance to change her mind, he entered her with one sure thrust and was surprised by the resistance that he met. Headley jerked under his body and let out a small cry of protest.

She tried to push him off her, but he pressed his chest to hers and planted small kisses down the side of her face.

He was stunned that Headley was still a virgin and proud that he was at first and only man to know her like this.

"Sweetheart, are you okay?" he whispered near her ear as he tried to let her get used to the feel of him inside of her body. He knew that he was a big man and he didn't want to scare her.

"It feels so strange," she whispered, squirming underneath his body. If Headley kept moving around like that, he would lose the last ounce of gentleman he had left inside of him.

His cock was painfully hard and he needed to find release with the only woman he had dreamt about for the past ten years.

Rich brown eyes stared into his as Headley traced his back with her fingertips. The sensation caused him to slowly start thrusting in and out of her tight body. A soft sound coming from Headley's mouth made him stop.

"Am I hurting you?" He didn't want to stop....he would rather cut off his right arm not to, but even now, if Headley told him to stop, he would respect her wishes.

"No," she whimpered pulling at his hips. "You feel so good inside of me. I want more...can I please have more?"

"Shit....!" Troy growled before he pushed his aching cock deeply into Headley's tightness.

It had been so long since he had been with a woman like this that he almost lost control when Headley's teeth started to nibble at his ear.

Capturing her lips with his, he crushed her to him while his body pushed deeply into hers. Troy kept his eyes open while Headley's were closed tight. He didn't want to miss a minute of this.

Her warm brown skin looked so unbelievable underneath his. The contrast in their skin tones only added to the erotic picture she made, heightening his need to make Headley his forever.

Sweat dripped from his body down onto Headley's equally sweating one.

Bending down, he licked the moisture from the valley between her breasts but his body never lost its tempo.

Her inner muscles clamped down his cock, pulling him even deeper into her body and he knew at that moment that Headley was meant to be his wife.

Headley was trying to think of anything but how good Troy felt and the magic he was working on her body.

Opening her eyes a little, she saw how handsome Troy looked above her with his dark hair plastered to his head from sweat.

How his strong jaw was clenched as he concentration on making love to her. The manly scent of him was almost her undoing at his thick tongue licked at her breasts.

God, she wouldn't be able to leave him after this. Her body was being seduced by his and she didn't give a damn if it was. Wrapping her legs around his hips, she raised her hips to meet Troy thrust for thrust.

"Troy," she whispered, then moaned softly.

Blue eyes locked with hers as Troy slowed his movements. "Say you'll marry me."

"What?" Headley shook her head trying to clear the trance Troy had placed her in.

"I want you to agree to marry me," he repeated thrusting in and then pulling back out.

"I can't."

"Yes, you can and you will," Troy uttered as he pushed his penis back into Headley waiting body. "I won't take no for an answer."

He wasn't going to let Headley get out of this. She wasn't going to win the bet, so she would have to marry him anyway. This would just happen sooner than she thought.

"Say yes," he uttered in a demanding growl.

"Yes?"

Finally, he thought.

"Now, tell me like you mean it." Troy pumped into her with another amazing thrust.

"YES!" Headley screamed as her orgasms rocked through her body.

The pleasure was pure and explosive as Troy found his release seconds after Headley. Headley's soft warmth beneath him helped his orgasm last longer than it ever had in the past. A deep feeling of peace entered his soul as he planted soft kisses on Headley's face.

"That was out of this world. I never felt like this before," Troy confessed as pulled out of Headley.

He cupped her face in his hands and stared into her wonderful eyes. "You know that you agreed to marry me, right? I'm not going to let you back out."

Headley moistened her lips with her tongue. "I remember. I won't back out on my word."

Troy wasn't pleased with himself, but this was the only way he could insure that Headley would be his. She may not be head over heels in love with him, but that could come with time.

"Hmmm....when do you want to get married....a year?"

His blue eyes never left hers for an instant. "No way I'm waiting that long to marry you, sweetheart. We're getting married in three days."

Chapter Eleven

"Three days," Headley shrieked, jumping up from the lounge chair pulling her dress around her body. "Have you lost your mind? I can't marry you in three days. What will people think...hell, what will they say?"

She got dressed as quickly as she could as she tried to think of a way out of this mess. She couldn't marry Troy that soon. She had to get herself under control first, find a way to conceal her emotions when it came to the hunk in front of her.

No....three days wouldn't give her enough time to accomplish that.

"Do you think I care about people's opinions? I'm going to marry you in seventy-two hours if I've to carry you kicking and screaming down the aisle. You aren't backing out of this. You would have to marry me next month anyway, so why do a couple of weeks make any difference?"

Headley couldn't take all of this. She was still trying to process the fact she just slept with him and didn't use a condom. What if she was pregnant? Lord...she needed time to think and seeing Troy's sculptured, naked body wasn't helping her at all. She needed time away from him to clear her head.

"I still think getting married in three days is wrong. You aren't thinking clearly. After we've both had time to get our focus back and realize it was just sex, things will be much clearer."

Troy took a step towards her. His eyes blazed with sudden anger as he grabbed her by the arms and jerked her to his body. "We didn't just have sex. We made love and nothing you can think about doing will change that fact. You might think

146

you're too good to have my penis inside of your body, but it happened. So you'll going to have to deal with it because I'm going to make love to you a lot after we're married. This sure in the hell isn't going to be a marriage in name only."

What was Troy talking about? She wasn't ashamed about what happened. She was only scared about him finding out she was in love with him. How could he possibly think she would want a sexless marriage?

"Listen, I think..."

"No, you listen," Troy growled cutting her off. "I want you to get everything you need to get done in the next couple of days because you're doing to be my wife. Any clothes or items you want brought from your father's house over here, do it. But you will be living under the same roof as me. I don't want any arguments about it, Headley."

"You can't tell me what to do. You aren't the ruler of me," she snapped.

Her emotions were out of control. She hated Troy one minute then a split second later she wanted him to kiss her senseless.

"You want to bet," he growled before his mouth took control of hers. Long fingers quickly untied the front of her dress and Troy's large hand cupped her ass. Lifting her up, he entered her with one thrust, filling her with his thickness.

He didn't give her time to react before he was moving her up and down his massive cock. Groaning in the back of her throat, Headley wrapped her arms around Troy's neck.

Walking with her in his arms, Troy pressed her back against the wall near the sliding doors that lead inside the house and continued his sensual assault on her body.

"You're mine and I'm never going to give you up," he breathed into her mouth as his hand tightened on her ass.

Headley wanted so badly to hate what Troy was doing to her, but she loved every damn minute. Troy knew her body better than she did. "Say that you belong to me," he demanded, withdrawing then entering her again.

"No."

Enter

Withdraw

"Headley, say it," Troy growled then nibbled at her earlobe while his hips kept their steady pace.

"I'm not going to," she moaned.

Enter

Withdraw

Enter

Withdraw

149

"Yes, you will," he swore and he dropped his head and drew a nipple into his mouth, biting it gently. His body imprisoned hers in a web of growing arousal and she wouldn't be able to deny the truth much longer.

Troy licked her nipple before he raised his head and his amazing eyes connected with hers. "Last chance for you to say it," he whispered as his thrusts increased while he pressed her chest to his.

Skin to skin, they were as one. She couldn't hold back any longer.

"YES! I belong to you!" Headley screamed as her orgasm ripped through her body.

"Finally," Troy muttered as he gave her another deep thrust before spilling his seed into her body.

Headley sighed as Troy planted soft kissed on her face and neck as he slid her down his body until her feet touched the ground. She wanted to say something to push him away, but she couldn't.

Instead, she abandoned herself to the feeling of satisfaction that Troy had left with her.

How was she going to be married to this man and not want him every moment of the day? Hell....she was already over her head and she wasn't even married to him yet.

"Are you okay?" Troy asked, fixing her dress. "Was I too rough with you?"

The concern in his voice almost made her cry. It sounded so sincere and sweet. "No, I'm fine." She replied moving away so she could put some space between the two of them.

Going back over to the chair, she slipped her shoes back on and brushed her hair out of her face. They had reached the point of no return now. There was no going back to the way things used to be.

She shivered as Troy wrapped his arms around her waist and planted a kiss on the back of her neck. "Don't withdraw from me. What happened between was perfection and I don't want any second thoughts running around in that gorgeous head of yours."

"I'm not having second thoughts," she lied, unwrapping Troy's arms from her body. "I just need to go home, take a shower and visit my dad at the hospital."

Headley eased away from the warm body behind her and hurried towards the sliding glass doors.

"If you wait for me to take a quick shower and get dressed, I'll take you home and then to visit Douglas."

Pausing in the open doorway, Headley shook her head but didn't glance back over her shoulder at Troy. She wouldn't be able to leave if she saw his naked body again.

"No, I want to go by myself. I'll talk to you later."

She dashed inside the house and then out the front door before he could stop her.

Chapter Twelve

"Ms. Rose, can I speak to you for a moment?" The nurse asked her as soon as she stepped off the elevator. Her heart dropped to the bottom of her feet as all kinds of thoughts raced through her mind. Had something happened to her father and she missed the phone call because she was with Troy? She would never forgive herself if that were the case.

"Is there something wrong with my father?" She whispered scared to hear the answer.

"No, honey," the nurse smiled. "It's good news. He opened his eyes today."

"He's awake?"

"Yes....he's awake, but he's still a little out of it. Still, the doctor said he should make a full recovery."

"He isn't going to have any of the side effects a heart attack usually causes?" Headley frowned. "I thought most heart attack patients have some sort of setback, especially without therapy."

The nurse nodded. "Your father is going to need a lot of therapy in the future, but although his speech was slow, it was clear and the doctor understood every word that he said."

Headley blinked back tears of joy. "This is wonderful news. Can I go and see him?"

"Yes, but he might be asleep," the nurses told her, "because the doctor just got through examining him. You're welcome to stay with him."

"I would like that a lot." She touched the nurse on the arm and then hurried to her father's room. She couldn't have gotten better new today.

Poking her head inside the door, Headley noticed that her father was breathing without all the tubes that were usually present. She came completely into the room and took a seat at his bedside. "I'm so glad you're better," she whispered taking his hands in hers.

For the moment, Troy and her feelings for him were taking a back seat. She knew she had a wedding coming up, but right now she wanted this time with her father.

"I don't believe you," Maxwell said reaching for the glass that Fancy placed in front of him. He tried not to notice how she didn't give him her usually perky smile and wink. Instead she smiled at Troy and Cole then left without a second glance in his direction.

He shouldn't feel jealous, but he did. What was wrong with him now? She used to love flirting with him. Now all she did was pawn him off on other waitress at the Tycoon's club. If she saw him coming, she would turn and go the other way.

"Max, if you're done staring at Fancy, can you pay attention to me?" Troy laughed next to him.

"I wasn't staring at Fancy," he lied and then took a swallow of his drink.

"Sure you weren't," Cole snickered. "You haven't taken your eyes off her all night. We're here to help Troy with his problems. After we get him married off to his long-time love, then we can help you get the adorable Fancy."

"Are you sure that you want to marry Headley? She hasn't given you anything but trouble since she waltzed back into town," Maxwell complained.

Troy knew why Maxwell wanted to stay a bachelor, something not even Cole was privileged enough to know the truth about. Of course, he wasn't about to let it out in the open now. However, he was in love with Headley and being married to her was his only dream now.

"Listen, I'm getting married in three days, and I want the both of you to be there. Headley is still trying to fight me on this, but it isn't going to work. After today we have to get married."

"What happened? Did you sleep with her?" Cole laughed and then stopped when he tossed his friend a hard look.

"Damn, I never thought Headley would ever give you a taste of her forbidden fruit," Maxwell uttered as he raised his hand to order another drink.

"Keep bad mouthing my fiancée and see what happens to you," Troy threatened. "I'm not going to put up with your shit when it comes to Headley. Both of you know how I feel about her and nothing is going to stop me from marrying her."

Maxwell stopped talking to him when Fancy came back to take his drink order. "What can I get you, Mr. Reed?" She asked.

"I want another bourbon and bring us another bowl of peanuts," Maxwell answered. He noticed how his buddy was looking at Fancy, but she didn't seem to care. She kept glancing at him for some odd reason.

"Fancy, is there something you want to say to me?" Troy inquired.

"I'm just surprise that you're here with everything that's going on with Headley," she shrugged.

"What's wrong with Headley? Is she hurt?"

"No, you haven't heard? I thought she would have called you."

"Headley didn't call me. Tell me what's happened to her," he snapped coming around the table.

Fancy pressed her pad to her breasts and took a step back from him. "You don't have to yell at me, Mr. Christian."

Taking a deep breath, Troy calmed himself. Fancy was right, he shouldn't have yelled at her. "I apologize. Can you please tell me what's wrong with Headley?"

"Nothing is wrong with her. She just called and told me a few minutes ago that her father woke up at the hospital and the doctor thinks he's going to make a full recovery."

"Douglas is awake?" Troy asked hating the feeling that came to his gut.

This couldn't be happening to him!

Not when he was so close to getting everything that he wanted. Headley was almost his, and Douglas was going to ruin it. There was no way in hell that man would let Headley marry him.

"Yeah, and Headley is so happy. You should have heard her on the phone. Are you going to see her?"

"Hmm….no," he replied. "I think I should let Headley have this time with Douglas. I'm going home. I've got some things that I have to take care of." He eased past Fancy, but he felt her eyes as well as his friends on his back until he walked out the door.

As he walked to his truck, Troy blocked out the cold air. All he could think about was getting Headley to marry him before Douglas got out of the hospital. He hated to lose. He wasn't allowing Headley to slip through his fingers. He loved her too *damn* much to let that happen.

Getting inside his truck, he drummed his fingers on the steering wheel while his mind thought of a way to get Headley before Douglas had a chance to poison her against him.

"I'm worth a hell of a lot of money and it's about time I start using some of it." Troy dug his cell phone out of his jeans pocket and punched in a number. He waited until the person answered and then barked out his order.

"I need you at my home within the hour. I have something that demands your attention."

Chapter Thirteen

Headley stood outside of Troy's house and debated on whether or not she should go inside.

So many things had changed between them within the past twenty-four hours. She had made love to him, twice, and now she was supposed to get married to him.

How could all of this have taken place so suddenly? Her childhood dream had been to marry the handsome older guy who lived across the field from her, and now it might be happening.

Chewing on her bottom lip, she got herself under control and knocked on the door. She wanted to walk right on in, but after what happened the last time she thought it might be better to knock first.

She waited a few minutes for someone to come to the door but when no one did, she decided to let herself in. "Troy, are you here?" Headley yelled closing the door behind her. "We need to talk."

The quietness of the house was a little eerie to her. There was usually some kind of noise around, usually coming from Troy's staff, but tonight it was dead silence. She thought twice about moving further into the room.

"Troy, if you're here, I really need to speak to you. It's very important." She wandered into the living room and stopped at the sight she found. The entire place had been changed into a beautiful setting. Several candles were lit everywhere, white roses lined the fireplace and the tables around the room. A man she had never seen before was standing in the center of the room looking at her.

"What's going on?" Headley asked taken back. However, the man only smiled at her and pointed behind her.

Spinning around, she gasped at the sight of Troy positioned in the open doorway. He looked eye-popping gorgeous in a black tux with a white rose in his lapel. "Headley, I'm glad you came on your own. I thought I might have to call you," he said coming towards her.

"Troy, what is all of this about?" She whispered.

"You don't know," he uttered, stopping in front of her.

Headley shook her head. "No. I don't have a clue."

"It's our wedding night."

"That's impossible. We aren't getting married tonight. Our wedding is three days from now."

"Not anymore," Troy answered pulling her against his chest. "I'm not going to wait any longer to marry you. I know you Headley. You'll get cold feet and run out on me. So, I paid the good judge here to marry us tonight without the blood tests. We can get those later."

Planting her hands against Troy's hard chest, Headley shoved him away from her. He couldn't do this to her. She wasn't ready to get married tonight.

Troy was fine earlier in the day with them waiting, so what was with the rush now? Was there something going on that she didn't know about?

"I can't marry you tonight."

"Sweetheart, you don't have a say in this discussion. We're getting married tonight. Now just take a deep breath and it will be okay. I've taken care of everything."

"This isn't making any sense," she muttered moving away from Troy and the tempting scent of his cologne. "We have to talk about this. I need to tell you something."

"You can tell me anything you want after we say I do," Troy exclaimed wrapping his arms around her waist.

Think of a way out of this!

"I can't marry you," she said.

"Why not?" Strong lips pressed against the side of her neck while long fingers massaged her stomach through her shirt.

"I don't have a dress to wear."

"Yes, you do," he stated stepping back from her. "Go upstairs and it's the first door on your left. Everything you need is up there and I'm giving you thirty minutes to get ready. If you aren't back by then, I'll come up there and get you."

"Troy...." Headley retorted facing the man, she was in love with.

"Headley, don't make me carry you up those stairs. This is your last night as a single woman. Now, you can either go up those stairs or I can carry you up them, but you're going to marry me tonight."

"I'm going." She stepped around Troy's powerful body and headed up the stairs wondering why he was so insistent on marrying her tonight. However, if Headley had looked back at the man in the living room, the answer to her question was written all over his face.

Chapter Fourteen

Resting his hand in his palm, Troy watched his new wife as she slept soundly next to him. She was shocked by the surprise wedding just as he knew she would be, but he wasn't going to take the chance of losing her again.

Douglas was awake and her father *hated* him. He could have been married to Headley years ago if she hadn't run from him.

She would be so surprised to know how much he cared about her. Headley could have him wrapped around her little finger if she wanted to.

Brushing a strand of hair off her forehead, he ran the tip of his finger down her smooth cheek.

She still looked so much like the young woman he fell in love with. A part of him was upset she didn't return his feelings, but it didn't matter. Headley was his now and nothing was going to change that.

Easing the covers off her body, he tossed them over the side of the bed. He had been so busy earlier loving his wife that he didn't get a chance to just look at her beautiful body.

Headley's skin was the most amazing shade of Hershey's kiss chocolate.

A sense of pride filled him knowing that she would never know another man's touch but his.

Her blemish free complexion would make any skin cream model jealous and Headley didn't even know it.

She was clueless to her natural beauty and sex appeal. She wasn't the type to go around and flaunt what she had. Headley was very low-key which only made her beauty stand out more.

Headley had a huge amount of dark, thick hair that he loved running his fingers through while they made love. He would hate it if she ever cut it short. On the rare occasions that she wore it down, it stopped in the middle of her back.

His eyes slowly traveled over her perky breasts down to her slightly curved stomach, where he gently laid his hand so he wouldn't wake Headley.

"I would love for you to be pregnant. A baby would only seal the love I've for you," he whispered. They had not used protection even once since they started making love.

Troy removed his hand and pulled Headley flush against his body, because he couldn't fathomed one night without her wrapped in his arms. "I hope that one day you will love me as much as I love you."

"I'm going into town. I'll be back in a couple of hours," Headley yelled at him as glanced up from the stack of papers on his desk.

"Wait a minute. Come back here."

"What is it?" Headley asked coming back into his office. "I need to go or I'm going to be late."

Troy's eyes narrowed on the red t-shirt that his wife was wearing. "I know you aren't going where I think you are." He got up from behind the table and advanced towards Headley.

"Yeah....Tommy gave me my job back at the Tycoon's Club. Fancy is sick and he needed someone to fill in for her. I've got to go or I'm going to be late." Headley turned to leave, but he caught her by the arm and then let go when she gave him a look.

"My wife isn't going to work in that place dressed like that. I won't allow it." Crossing his arms over his chest, Troy dared Headley to deny him.

He had enough money from all of his investment ventures that she never had to work a day in her life. She was his wife now and she wasn't going to step foot back in that club.

All those men there were only looking for one thing and they weren't going to find it with Headley.

"You can't be serious," she gasped staring up at him. "My best friend needs my help and you're demanding that I ignore her and Tommy's request for help. I don't believe you. If it was Maxwell or Cole you would be out that door in a matter of seconds. Hell, you wouldn't even tell me goodbye before you left."

"It's different. My friends would only come to me for help when they really needed it. Fancy is always in some kind of trouble and most people here just blew it off. But now that you're back in town, she has you to run to. Once you learn how to tell her no, things will be a lot better."

"Listen Troy, just because we're married now doesn't mean that you own me. I'm still my own person and I can do what I want. Fancy needs my help and I'm going to help her." Turning away from him, Headley stormed for the door but she didn't make it two steps.

He wrapped his hand around her arm and tugged her back to him. Tossing her over his shoulder, Troy carried his struggling wife from the room.

"Troy, you put me down this instant," she screamed hitting him in the back. "You know how much I hate when you do this."

"You aren't going to leave the house dressed in that outfit. I know what the men at the Tycoon's Club are looking for and they aren't going to get it from my wife," he growled as he headed up the stairs.

"Do you really think I'm going there to do something like that? Do you not trust me?"

174

Troy blocked out the hurt in Headley's voice as he opened the bedroom door and carried her inside. She didn't get how men were drawn to her. She was so damn sexy without even trying. He knew the thoughts that raced through his mind when he first saw Headley in that outfit. .

Sliding Headley down his body, he held her in front of him so she wouldn't move away. "Sweetheart, I trust you. However, the men at the club are the ones I don't trust. I know they would find a way to touch that unbelievable body of yours and then I would have to hurt one of them. Honestly, I'm not interested in spending the night in jail but I would do it for you."

"You have control issues," Headley uttered shaking off his touch, "and I'm not going to stay here and feed into this nonsense. I'm going to the club and I'll be home in a couple of hours." She moved around his body to leave, but he stepped in front of her.

"No, you aren't." Walking to the door, he stood there blocking her exit.

Headley might hate him for this, but he didn't care. The Tycoon's Club was no place for his wife and he was going to make sure she stayed home.

"Just stay here and watch some television. After I'm finished with my work downstairs, we can go out and talk about a more suitable place for you to find a job. I don't think you need to work, but if you really want to, I won't stop you."

"You aren't thinking about leaving me locked in this room. I know you aren't." Headley took a step towards him.

"I'll be back." Troy stepped out into the hallway and closed the door, locking it quickly behind him.

"Troy Christian, you get your ass back here this minute and unlock this damn door. You can't keep me from helping out Fancy." The sound of his wife's fists banging on the door echoed in the hallway.

"Fancy is a grown woman and it's time for her to deal with her own problems. You aren't her problem-solver, so calm down. I'll be back before you know it." Troy touched the door with his hand and then left, more than a little concerned about how he was going to make this up to Headley.

Moving away from the door, Headley threw out curses that would have embarrassed the most seasoned sailor. "I can't believe this! He actually locked me in this room like I was a child." She had to find a way out of here.

Troy wasn't going to have this kind of power over her. He might be her husband now, but that didn't make him the ruler of her world.

If she didn't love him so damn much, she would be headed to a lawyer's office tomorrow.

They had only been married for a week and he was losing his mind.

She had a right to help out any of her friends without him saying a word. He would have to learn how to be more supportive of her choices or their marriage wasn't going to work.

She had loved this bad boy side of him when she was a teenager. It made him so much more dangerous to fantasize about; however, now that she was older it wasn't as hot.

Why are you lying to yourself? You know that you find that 'Me Tarzan and you Jane' stuff a turn-on. Troy had a way of making his domineering personality a sexy little game between the two of them.

She honestly didn't mind it sometimes, but today wasn't one of those days. Her friend was in trouble and she wasn't going to let Fancy down.

"I've got to find a way out of here. Troy isn't going to get away with this."

Pacing around the room, Headley tried to think of ways to escape when her eyes landed on the window.

"Yes!" She grinned as she rushed over to it.

She undid the front latch and pushed it open. Looking over the edge, she tried not to think about how high she was up. There was no way she could jump out without hurting herself. The drop would be too much. However, the big oak tree next to the window would be the perfect thing for her to climb down.

Standing on the ledge, she grabbed one of the branches and swung her body around the limb. She pushed her fear to the back of her mind as she quickly climbed down the tree and jumped down at the bottom.

Troy was going to hit the roof when he found out that she was gone, but it couldn't be helped. He had to understand that she wasn't a piece of property that he could lock away anytime he desired.

"I'll deal with Troy when I get back. I know he's going to be pissed, but I can't worry about that now." Headley muttered as she made a dash for one of the cars parked in the driveway.

She just hoped the car keys were inside of the glove compartment or her mission impossible escape would have been for nothing.

Chapter Fifteen

"Mr. Christian, your wife is on the phone. Do you want me to put her call through?" Heather asked him. "This is the third time that she has called."

"No, tell her that I'm still in a meeting and I'll call her when I get out." Troy pushed the disconnect button on his phone and ran his hand down his face.

He was still pissed that Headley actually climbed out the window to go and help Fancy. She could have broken her neck and his life would have been over.

Why couldn't she just listen to him? He wasn't ready to talk to her yet.

"Are you still mad at Headley?" Cole asked. "You shouldn't hold a grudge over something so small. Headley was just being a good friend."

"Cole, if I wanted your opinion, I would ask for it. Headley knew that I didn't want her back at the club and she went anyway. She defied me and I'm not pleased at all."

"Have you listened to yourself at all? Headley is your wife. You've been in love with this woman for most of your life, but you aren't acting like it. You can't control her by barking out orders or making demands on her."

Troy *hated* that Cole was right, but it was hard for him to share Headley now that she was finally married to him. He just wanted them to stay locked away with each other, but in reality he knew that wouldn't happen.

"I hear what you're saying, but she acted like I was holding her prisoner in our house."

"Man, what would you call it if she locked you in the bedroom and told you not to leave? Headley is a wonderful woman. Maxwell and I would both give our right arm to find someone like her, but you're going to lose her if you keep this up."

Fear lodged his words in his throat. Headley wouldn't leave him over their first fight. He would tell her that under no certain terms was that an option. Wait!

Talking to her like that would make him a divorced man. He had to find a better way to communicate with his wife. He was just so used to barking out orders.

"Cole, I love Headley so much. I don't want to lose her. Hell, we haven't even been married for two weeks and I'm already acting like a jerk."

"You're in love and maybe if she knew that, things would be so much clearer for her. But if you kept it a secret, she'll never tell you how she feels," Cole commented.

"I know one thing for sure. Headley isn't in love with me. She just married me to get her father out of debt and because the sex is good between us." He wished like hell that his wife was in love with him.

"Are you seriously that dumb?"

"What are you talking about? Why are you calling me names?"

Cole stared at him closely before shock registered on his friend's face. "You honestly don't know, do you?"

"Know what?" Troy frowned. "I don't have a clue what you're talking about."

"Headley is in love with you," Cole uttered, shocked.

"Sure she is and that's why I've been sleeping in the guest room for the past two days."

"First, do you honestly think Headley would have married you if she wasn't in love with you? Does she come off like a woman who would do that to settle a money debt her father owed? How many times did she suggest using any kind of protection when the two of you made love before you got married?"

Hope filled Troy's chest as Cole's words started to sink in. "Why hasn't she told me?"

"Have you given her a chance to say anything? I know you and how you work when it comes to business. You probably approached the marriage proposal like a business deal. I bet you have never told her you love her to see what she would even say. And the reason you're in the guest room is all your fault. Did Headley tell to go there or was your pride hurt and you took it out on her?"

"How did you get so damn smart?" he asked. Cole was like Maxwell, he didn't know much about his friend's past or any past loves in his life.

"Let's just say I learned from experience and I don't want to see you lose the love of your life. Now, if I were you, I would find a way to make up with her and fast."

"Do you think it's too late?" His wife might not be open to listening to him after he blew off her latest phone call.

"If you don't do anything else to hurt her, I think you should be fine. But remember, tell her that you love her and find a way to make her understand that you're telling her the truth."

"Wish me luck," Troy sighed.

"I do wish you luck, because you're going to need it," Cole answered.

Chapter Sixteen

"I never guessed that not taking your phone calls would make you pack up your clothes," Troy joked as he came into his bedroom. His heart was breaking. Cole was right, Headley was going to leave him if he didn't act fast and find the words to make her stay.

"Troy, I'm leaving you. I've tried talking to you, but you just don't know how to listen without giving orders. I'm fed up with it." Headley folded up a couple of shirts and added them to the suitcase on the bed.

"Headley, we've only been married for a week. We're just getting used to each other. I don't think you should leave and move back to your dad's house. Just give it some more time and we'll get through this."

"Did you not hear what I said?" she asked, pausing in folding up the rest of her clothes. "I'm going back home."

"Yeah....I heard you say that you're going back to your father's house. I don't think you should. We can't work things out if you are there and I'm here. We need to be under the same roof and talk this thorough."

"You do not understand what I'm telling you," she sighed shaking her head. "When I said I'm going home, I meant back to New York. I called and talked to Avant and he offered me my job back with a raise. The hospital is getting my father's paperwork ready so I can take him with me."

New York!!!

Headley was leaving Texas forever. How could Cole think she was ever in love with him? She would never do this if she had any love in her heart for him.

"Why are you doing this?" He demanded. "I have money, power and I know I'm a nice-looking man. What is so special about New York that you want to leave me? I can give you a good life and you're throwing it all back in my face."

"DAMN IT!" Headley snapped, shocking the hell out of him.

He never had seen her this upset before. Even when she was mad at him about her father, she never yelled at him.

"Why is it always about you? How do you think I feel being in a marriage where I love my husband and all he thinks about is money, power and a way to keep me under his thumb? I can't do this anymore."

"I've been in love with you since I saw you talking to your father on the steps in front of your house the first day you moved to town. All I thought about was being a part of your life. When I got the letter from my father telling me to come here and talk to you, I thought it might mean something different, but the letter I got from you a few days later proved him wrong."

Headley loved him! He wanted to tell her he felt the same way, but she wouldn't stop talking long enough to let him.

"How could I even think that maybe after we got married your feelings would change for me? Men like you live on power, not love. I won't stay in a place like this. I want to be in love and have someone who I will enjoy seeing each and every day."

"Headley, if you just listen, I've got something to tell you," Troy exclaimed as he made his way over to his wife.

God, he couldn't keep the silly grin off his face.

All he wanted to do was knock that damn suitcase off the bed and make love to his gorgeous wife for the rest of the night.

Hell, he might take off the rest of the month and take her on a honeymoon.

"No, stay away from me Troy," Headley said holding up her hand. "I don't want to hear a word that you've got to say. It's over and I only want to finish packing up my stuff so I can leave."

"I can't let you leave me," he whispered wrapping his hand gently around Headley's wrist. He kissed each fingertip and then placed her hand over his heart.

"You can't tell me what to do anymore, Troy." She said looking into his eyes and the sadness he saw there, cut him to the core. He had a lot of stuff to make up for.

"Okay...how about I ask the woman that I'm crazy in love with to stay and forgive me for being an asshole to her since she came back to town?"

Headley gasped and her eyes lit up for a moment only to go right back out.

"Troy, nice try, but I don't believe you. Did you think I had forgotten about how you told me that you hated to lose? You're just using the love card to make me stay. Nothing will change if I do. I'll still be this possession you can't let out of your sight."

Troy sighed heavily, his voice filled with despair. "I know that I haven't ever given you any reason to believe that I love you, but I do. I love you so much that I'm willingly to let your father move in here with us."

"Hell, if you still want to do fashion design in New York, I'll have my pilot fly you back and forth every day. But I can't lose you. I let you walk out of my life ten years ago and I've regretted it ever since."

Were his words too late? Had he ruined something in a week that he had waited to get for the past ten years of his life? Headley had to give him a second chance. He would do anything she asked, just as long as she didn't leave him.

"You really love me enough to let my father move in her with us?" She asked wrapping her arms around his neck.

"Yes...hell, he can move in right now to our room. I'm willingly to do anything to show you how much I love you, Mrs. Christian." Troy wanted to wrap Headley up in his arms and kiss her senseless, but he wasn't sure if she was ready for that or not.

Titling her head to the side, Headley looked at him with such love in her eyes that it almost brought him to his knees.

"Troy, you really make it hard for a woman to love you and I was almost out the door until Cole called and stopped me."

"What does Cole have to do with this?" he frowned.

"Cole told me that I had to do something to shock you into admitting how much you cared about me," she grinned kissing him lightly on the mouth.

A thought popped into Troy's head as he picked up his wife and carried her over the bed. Holding her against his chest, he knocked her suitcase off with his free hand and laid her down on the bed.

"Did you know about his trip to my office today?" He asked as his fingers worked on the front of her blouse.

"Of course I did. Who do you think put him up to it?" she grinned. "I made a bet with him."

"What kind of bet was it?" Hell, he didn't care what it was. He would pay Cole anything he wanted now that he had the woman he loved wrapped up in his arms.

"I bet him that you would spend the next forty years making me the happiest woman in the world."

Stripping the shirt off his gorgeous wife's body, Troy tossed it to the floor. "Sweetheart, that's one bet I don't mind fulfilling each and every day for the rest of my life," he uttered as he captured Headley's lips with his.

The End

More about Marie Rochelle:

Marie Rochelle is a bestselling author of interracial romances featuring black women and white men. Marie first started writing IR books about two years ago and it has been nonstop for her ever since. Her first best selling IR romance was entitled Taken by Storm. In addition, Marie has a very successful series called The Men of CCD and right now she's working on the much awaited third book in the series: Tempting Turner. Marie has enjoyed writing from a very young age and is happy she decided to turn her career toward the IR market; a market that she had enjoyed for years herself. She has always dreamt of being a writer and now is truly happy to see her dreams becoming a reality.

To find out more about her visit her web site: www.freewebs.com/irwriter

Marie Rochelle books Coming Soon

Books out or coming soon:

Red Rose Publishing:

Beneath the Surface-Available Now

Pamper Me- Available Now

Be With you – Available Now

Cover Model – Available Now

With all my Heart – Available Now

Love Play – Coming Soon

Tycoon Club Series

Blindsided

Cobblestone Press

Special Delivery- Available Now

Phaze

All The Fixin- Available Now

My Deepest Love

Outlaw: Caught

A Taste of Love: Richard

Loving True – Coming Soon

Taken by Storm- Coming

Stay tuned for mo

Marie Rochelle fro1

Here is a list of her k

Beneath the Surface

Pamper Me

Be With you

Cover Model

With all my Heart

Love Play – Coming Soc

Tycoon Club Series

Dangerous Bet: Troy's R

Blindsided

Made in the USA
Lexington, KY
04 October 2010